ELF

A Junior Novel

ELF

A Junior Novel

Adapted by Ellen Weiss

PSS!
PRICE STERN SLOAN

Cover photo: Peter Tangen / © 2003 New Line Productions
Insert photos: Alan Markfield and Michael Gingsburg / © 2003 New Line Productions

Published by Price Stern Sloan, a division of Penguin Young Readers Group,
345 Hudson Street, New York, NY 10014.
PSS! is a registered trademark of Penguin Group (USA) Inc.

ISBN 0-8431-0771-5   A B C D E F G H I J

Prologue

by Papa Elf

Elves love to tell stories. You probably didn't know that, did you? Well, there are a lot of things about elves that people don't know. For instance, elves can not tell a lie. It's physiologically impossible.

Here's another interesting elf fact: There are only three jobs available to an elf.

You can make shoes at night while an old cobbler sleeps, but it's not exactly the most rewarding work. Especially when, as often as not, the cobbler's a lazy bum who can't even manage to make one clog.

You can bake cookies in a tree. But, as you can imagine, it's dangerous having an oven in an oak during the dry season.

But the third job. Well, the third job makes

being an elf worthwhile. Some call it "the show" or "the big dance." It's the profession every elf aspires to. And that's to build toys in Santa's workshop—dolls, toy horses, action figures, squirt guns, even X-Boxes™. It's a job only an elf can do. The nimble fingers, natural cheer, and active minds of elves are perfect for toy building.

And no human could ever do this work. Their hands are too big, and they tend to get testy when overworked. In fact, no human has ever set foot in Santa's workshop. That is, until about thirty years ago. And in case you haven't guessed it, that's where our story begins. It was back in 1968. A particularly successful Christmas . . .

The Biggest Elf

By the soft light of the flickering Christmas tree bulbs, a nurse was changing the diaper of a laughing ten-month-old baby.

"You're quite a giggler, aren't you?" she said, smiling, as she laid him gently down in his crib. "Well, it's time for night-night."

She tucked him in tenderly and tiptoed out of the room. "Merry Christmas, my angel," she whispered as she closed the door.

Alone now, the baby pulled himself to his feet, still laughing, and stood hanging on to the bars of his crib.

Across the room, in the fireplace, a pair of black boots dropped down from the chimney above, followed by a big man in a red suit. The baby's eyes lit up. He shook the bars of the crib.

Quickly, Santa crossed the room to the Christmas tree and began setting out presents.

Hearing an abrupt bang, he glanced over at the crib. The side was down. It was empty. Santa, not having noticed the baby in the first place, went back to work.

Meanwhile, the baby was gleefully skittering across the floor toward a large, fuzzy teddy bear in Santa's big red bag.

At last, the most important workday of the year was over. All the elves were gathered to celebrate another successful Christmas, and several of them started chanting for a speech. Santa, seated in his rocker, finally stood in recognition of the applause. Merrily, he gestured for quiet.

"All right . . . all right," he said, settling them down. "Well, we've had another successful year. We didn't forget Delaware, and Prancer was able to control his bladder over Baltimore."

In response to this news, a party horn blew, and everyone laughed. Santa cheerfully patted downward with his hands for quiet. "And now, after a lot of hard work, it's time for a vacation, starting now!" he declared. He shot his wrist out of his sleeve to look at his watch. Five seconds ticked off as the elves all rested their heads on their elbows.

"All right! Vacation's over!" Santa announced. "Back to work! Time to start preparations for next Christmas."

The elves cheered happily and immediately got back to work.

But wait—what was that sound? They all heard it. It was a sort of cooing noise.

"What in the name of Sam Hill. . . ?" said Santa.

There it was again. Definitely cooing.

Perplexed, Santa looked down at his bag. At that moment, a human baby, dressed only in a diaper, crawled out and smiled.

The elves stared in awestruck silence. Finally, two twin elves approached the strange visitor. They looked at the back of the baby's diaper. "'Little Buddy Diapers'," the first elf read aloud. "Its name is Buddy," he concluded. "He must've . . . "

". . . snuck in your sack at the orphanage," his twin brother finished. "What do we do, Santa?"

Santa looked befuddled. He had to make some sort of decision about this. But fortunately, when it came to babies, Santa was a pushover. So he decided that Buddy would stay with an older elf who had always wanted a child but had been so committed to building toys, he had forgotten to settle down.

Buddy was raised by Papa Elf, his adoptive father. My, how Papa Elf loved that boy. Though Buddy grew twice as fast, he wasn't any different from the other elf children . . . except, perhaps, that he was as big as Papa Elf when he was two. And, of course, when he got a little bigger, he was way, way, way better at basketball than the rest of the elves.

And though it was against the Code of Elves to lie, all agreed that, until Buddy asked them, no one was going to bring up the fact that he was actually a human being.

And so, Buddy grew up among the elves. At elf school, his larger-and-larger body wedged into a tiny elf desk, he would eagerly answer the teacher's questions.

". . . And before we learn how to build the latest

in extreme graphic chipset processors," she'd say, pointing to the blackboard, "let's recite the Code of Elves, shall we? Number one?"

"TREAT EVERY DAY LIKE CHRISTMAS!" the elf students would sing out.

"Number two?" the elf teacher went on.

"THERE'S ROOM FOR EVERYONE ON THE NICE LIST!" responded her students.

"Number three?"

"THE BEST WAY TO SPREAD CHRISTMAS CHEER IS SINGING LOUD FOR ALL TO HEAR!" they would chant happily, Buddy the loudest of all.

Ice hockey was the elves' favorite sport, and Buddy joined in with gusto. The other elves were happy to include him, in spite of the fact that it was a little dangerous for them. They'd all gather around him in the locker room after a game and reach up to slap him in the butt. "Good game, Buddy!" they'd say.

"Thanks!" he'd reply. Then he'd apologize to whomever he'd hurt.

"No sweat. It's just a collarbone!" they might reply cheerfully.

But as much as Buddy was accepted by his

friends and family, there were a few drawbacks to being a human in an elf's world.

There were the tiny doorways—wham!

There were the low ceiling beams—whump!

There were the open cabinet doors, right into the gut—crash!

There was even the problem of getting his feet tangled up in the elves' tiny Christmas tree ornaments, pulling the tree down, falling into the fireplace, and becoming engulfed in flames as the elves sprayed him with their teeny tiny fire extinguishers.

"Ow!" Buddy would yowl. "Jeez . . . yikes . . . golly . . . Charles Dickens!" And, for the very worst occasions: "Son of a Nutcracker!"

And nowhere were Buddy's differences more obvious than in Santa's toy shop. His enormous hands were simply not equal to the demands of the assembly line.

It all came to a head one day when Buddy sat on the line, making Etch A Sketches™ with wooden hammers, like all the other elves. The supervisor came down the line and stopped beside Buddy.

"Gee, I'm sorry, Ming Ming, I'm gonna come

in a little short of my quota today," Buddy apologized.

"It's okay, Buddy," said the kindly supervisor. "How many Etch A Sketches™ did you get finished?"

Buddy was about to answer, but his face crumpled as he fought back tears.

"How many, Buddy?" Ming Ming asked. "It's okay, you can tell me."

Really tearing up now, Buddy set his tiny wooden hammer to the side, revealing his box of finished toys. "I only made. . . eighty-five!" he wailed.

A shocked silence fell over the workshop. Eighty-five? He might as well have said zero. The elves all looked at one another, at a loss for words.

Ming Ming, the supervisor, recovered first. "Oh, don't worry about it, Buddy, this is a great start!" he said as heartily as he could. "You're only 915 off the pace."

"Oh, why don't you just say it, Ming Ming!" howled the anguished Buddy. "I'm the worst toy maker in the whole world! I'm a COTTON-HEAD NINNY MUGGINS!"

"Oh, you're not a cotton-head ninny muggins!"

the supervisor comforted him. "We all have different talents, that's all."

Buddy was not consoled. "Actually, it seems like everyone has the same talents—except for me."

"That's not true, you have lots of talents. Special talents . . . like, uh—" Ming Ming looked around to the other elves for backup. They chimed in, trying to help.

"You changed the batteries in the fire alarm!" offered one.

"You sure did! Triple A's!" said another, sounding ridiculously positive. "And in six months, you'll need to check 'em again! Won't he?" he asked everyone.

They all enthusiastically agreed.

"And you're the only baritone in the elf choir," someone else said. "You bring us down a whole octave!"

"In a good way!" added somebody else.

"See? You're not a cotton-head ninny muggins," said the supervisor triumphantly. "You're EX-traordinary!"

"Well, you know what?" Buddy blurted. "I'm sick

of being extraordinary!" He struggled to get his thighs out from under his desk and bolted from the room, tagging his head on the doorframe as he left.

Moments later, he stormed into the front door of his tiny house. A surprised Papa Elf looked up from his work as Buddy, so upset that he could not even speak, ran and locked himself in the bathroom.

The bathroom was absurdly small for Buddy, who was forced to squeeze in like Harry Houdini. The toilet was the size of a Big Gulp™ cup. Buddy sat on it and started to sob, washing his face in the tiny sink.

"Son? Are you okay?" asked Papa Elf, knocking tentatively at the door.

"Go away!"

"Buddy!" said Papa Elf, shocked. "Such violent language!"

Buddy, contrite, amended his outburst. "I'm sorry, Papa," he said. "May I please have some Buddy time?"

"Open up, son," said Papa Elf. "I think we need to talk."

The door finally creaked open, revealing the enormous figure of Buddy squeezed into the tiny room. Buddy wiggled out of the bathroom.

Papa Elf sat down on the sofa. "Come sit with your papa," he said. He winced as Buddy sat down on his knee. "All right, let's hear it," he said.

"Well, everyone knows you're Santa's Master Tinker," sniffled Buddy. "And Grandpapa was Master Tinker before you. And Great-Grandpapa before him. I'm supposed to follow in your footsteps . . . but I'm always letting everyone down."

"Well, there's something I should probably tell you, Buddy. And it's long overdue." Papa Elf took a deep breath. "You see . . . um. . . " he began.

"What is it, Papa?"

Papa Elf looked into Buddy's beautifully innocent eyes, and simply could not bring himself to do it. He chickened out and changed the subject. "I need your help on something," he said. "Up, up now, nice and—ow, OW!" he said, trying to shift Buddy's weight off his lap. "There we are."

Now Papa Elf led Buddy through the door to his workshop. And there, as big as life, was the most amazing sight Buddy had ever beheld. A magical glow emanated from its hand-rubbed, red-lacquered wood, lighting up the entire room.

"Wow!" Buddy gasped. "Santa's sleigh!" He reached toward it, and then hesitated. "Can I touch it?" he asked Papa Elf.

"Touch it? You're going to help me make it fly, Buddy."

"I thought the magical reindeers made the sleigh fly," said Buddy.

"And where do the reindeers get their magic from?" Papa Elf asked him.

"Christmas Spirit," Buddy replied. "Everyone knows that."

"Yes, but unfortunately, Christmas Spirit is becoming a very limited resource."

"What do you mean?" Buddy asked.

"Well, Buddy, as silly as it sounds, there are a lot of people down South who don't believe in Santa Claus." It was plain from the look on Papa Elf's face that it pained him to break the news to the innocent Buddy.

Buddy was naturally horrified. "What?" he said. "Who do they think puts their toys under the tree?"

"There's a rumor floating around that parents are putting them there."

"That's ridiculous! There's no way parents could do that all in one night! And what about Santa's cookies? I suppose parents eat them, too?" This was too ridiculous for Buddy even to absorb.

"I know. But every year, less and less people believe in Santa, and today we've got a real energy crisis on our hands. See how low the Claus-o-Meter is?" He showed Buddy a gauge on the instrument panel of the sleigh labeled, CHRISTMAS SPIRIT LEVELS. Its needle was resting in the red DANGEROUSLY LOW section. "That's why I installed this little baby back in the sixties," Papa Elf explained, pushing a red button. Immediately, a jet engine began to shudder with a high-pitched whir.

Buddy could not believe his eyes. "Oh, my gosh!" he cried.

"Watch the language, son," Papa Elf cautioned him.

"Forgive me, Papa. What's that?"

"A Viper turbojet with 358 cubic meters of

displacement, high-volume air intake, and customized spark timing," Papa Elf explained. Seeing Buddy's startled look, he added, "I know, it's a little less magical, but everyone's still getting their wish. That's the important thing, right?"

Papa Elf put his arm around Buddy. "Listen, the motor mounts are giving me some wiggle," he said. "Do you want to give the ol' man a hand?"

"Do I!" said Buddy, recovered from the shock of it all.

And just like that, father and son hunkered down and tinkered together. Crisis averted.

Time to Go

The next day, Buddy was on toy-testing duty in Santa's workshop. It was jack-in-the-box day, and he stood in front of a table full of them. He turned the crank on each toy in turn. Each one played "Pop! Goes the Weasel," and then the puppet popped out. Each time, Buddy was scared out of his wits.

POP! went the first one.

"AHH!" screamed Buddy.

POP! went the next one.

"Uhhh!!!" gasped Buddy.

The third one didn't pop for a moment; then, all of a sudden—*POP!*

"AAAHHHHH!" shrieked Buddy.

The whole experience was so harrowing, Buddy was wrung out. "I'm going to take five, okay, Ming Ming?" he said to the supervisor.

"Okay!" said Ming Ming cheerfully.

Buddy made his way to the kitchen, where elves took their breaks. Just as he was about to go in, he heard the voices of a few elves, who were drinking hot chocolate with peppermint sticks inside.

"And that EX-traor-dinary bit! That was quick thinking," said a voice Buddy recognized as Foom Foom's.

They were talking about him! They were talking behind his back!

"Hey, I feel bad for the guy. I just hope he doesn't get wise." It was Ming Ming, the supervisor!

"Hey, he's believed he's an elf for this long, hasn't he?" Foom Foom chuckled.

Buddy was numb with shock. Suddenly, his brain was flooded with flashbacks from his past: trying to squeeze into impossible little elf shoes at the shoemaker's; having to sleep on three elf beds pushed together; struggling to wash his hair under a three-foot-high shower head. And the choir, where no one came up higher than his belly button. And the doorways. And the beams. And the cabinets.

"Ow… jeez… yikes… golly… dickens… son of a Nutcracker!" Buddy murmured in response to the movie playing in his head.

Buddy did not go into the kitchenette. Instead, like the good elf he'd been trained to be, he plodded back to work and tried to block out the awful truth. He stood in the factory, staring blankly ahead of him as he tinkered with a Ken doll, moving its arms like his own arms. His head was spinning. He did not feel well. The room began to wheel, and his knees buckled.

His friend Pom Pom hurried over, concerned. "You don't look so good, Buddy. Are you okay?"

Buddy tried to speak, but instead he collapsed right on top of Pom Pom, crushing the little elf beneath his weight.

"I'm okay, Buddy!" said Pom Pom gamely, his voice muffled underneath Buddy. "Don't worry about a thing … I'm warm!"

A few hours later, Buddy awoke to find himself in Papa Elf's workshop. Papa was fussing over his son.

"Ooooooohhhh," Buddy groaned. "I had a terrible nightmare."

"What was it, Buddy?"

"I dreamt I wasn't an elf at all. I was a human. Oh, it was awful. I'm not a human, am I, Papa?" he asked.

"I knew this day would come. You see, Buddy, I love you and nothing can ever change that. But the fact is, it wasn't a dream. You're not like the rest of us," replied Papa Elf.

"You mean I'm not an elf?"

"No, son, you're a human being," said Papa Elf gravely.

"No wonder I'm always freezing!" yelled Buddy.

"We decided it was best to let you think you were one of us," Papa Elf explained.

"But I thought elves can't lie."

"We can't. But Buddy, you never asked! I thought for sure when you cracked six feet it would come up."

"I thought I had a glandular problem," said Buddy, getting upset now.

"Your glands are fine," he said.

"So, you're not my papa?" asked Buddy, his voice cracking with emotion as the full weight of the truth dawned on him.

"Oh, I'll always be your papa. It's just you have another papa, too," said Papa Elf. "A biological papa." He opened a drawer and showed Buddy a photo of a young couple obviously in love. He then proceeded to tell Buddy of how his father had fallen in love when he was very young with a beautiful girl named Susan Welles, how Buddy was born and put up for adoption by his mother, and how she had later passed away. He told Buddy that his father had never even known Buddy was born. And, most importantly, he told Buddy where his dad was: in a magical land called New York City.

Papa Elf put a snow globe down in front of Buddy. Inside was a tall, pointy building: the Empire State Building. NEW YORK CITY, the sign read.

Buddy was starting to have a meltdown. "Uhh!" he moaned. "I feel confused and sweaty! I need some Buddy time!"

And with that, he ran off.

"Buddy?! Buddy!" Papa Elf called after him. But Buddy was gone.

Buddy ran and ran. He passed some of his animal buddies: a rabbit, a raccoon, and a squirrel. They'd been his friends for so long, he did not even think it was odd that the animals could talk.

"Hey, Buddy!" called the raccoon. "Want to sing and pick snow berries?"

"Not now, Pipsy!" Buddy replied as he sped past.

In a little while he passed Fluffy the Snowman, another animated friend of his, in the front yard of a toasty little cottage.

"Hello, Buddy," called Fluffy.

"Oh. Hi, Fluffy," said Buddy in a dejected voice.

"Why the long face, partner?" Fluffy inquired.

"Well, it seems I'm . . . I'm . . . not an elf," Buddy replied.

"Of course you're not. You're six-two and had a beard when you were fifteen."

"Papa says my real father is living in a magical place far away," said Buddy. "I don't know what to do."

"At least you have a father. I was just rolled up one day. I never had anyone to play catch with. And even if I did, I only have sticks for arms."

"I guess I am pretty lucky after all," Buddy had to agree. "But I've never even left the North Pole."

"I bet your dad will be so happy to see you, he'll hug you and never let go," said Fluffy. "I wish I had a dad to hug. And even if I did, I only have sticks for arms."

Buddy's face took on a new look of determination. "I will!" he declared. "I'm gonna go find my dad!"

"Do all the things I never can," Fluffy called after Buddy as he sped off. "Hug him. And play catch. And scratch your behind."

❄ ❄ ❄

A little while later, Buddy took his last walk through the workshop. Each elf he passed said a choked-up good-bye.

"Bye, Choo-Choo!" said Buddy, also full of emotion. "Bye, Sunshine! Bye, Tinkle Winkle! Bye, Puffy! Bye, Vlade! Bye, Gayle!"

Now, in came the Big Guy himself. He stepped over to Buddy and put his arm around him. "So I hear you're going on a little journey to the big city?" said Santa Claus.

"Yeah," Buddy replied, "but I'm kind of nervous.

Fluffy the Snowman told me New York is really different."

"Don't listen to Fluffy," said Santa. "He's never been anywhere. He doesn't even have any feet. I've been to New York thousands of times."

"Wow. What's it like?"

"Well, there are some things you should know," Santa said. "If you see gum on the street, leave it there. It's not free candy. And there are, like, thirty Ray's Pizzas™ and they all say they're the original, but the real one's on Eleventh."

"So much to remember . . . " said Buddy, biting his lip.

"Don't worry, the climate should suit you. Something tells me this trip is going to be a good one when all is said and done." Santa patted him on the back. "It's time for my Buddy here to spread his wings," he said.

"I can't wait! Me and Dad are gonna go ice skating and eat sugarplums!" exclaimed Buddy.

"That's the other thing I wanted to talk to you about," said Santa, frowning. "You see, Buddy, your father . . . well, he's on the Naughty List."

"Nooooo!!!" gasped Buddy.

"I'm sorry, but it's true," said Santa sadly.

"My stomach hurts. It feels like evil," Buddy moaned.

"Listen, Buddy," said Santa, "some people, they get mixed up about what's important in life. But that doesn't mean they can't change. Maybe your dad just needs a little Christmas Spirit!"

Buddy brightened right up. "I'm good at that!" he said.

"I know you are."

Now Papa Elf stepped forward, trying to hide the fact that his eyes were filling with tears. He gave Buddy a hug. "I love you, Buddy," he said. "And I'll always be here for you." Now he was really bawling. "Now go on, get!" he said, turning his face away.

"Yes, Papa," said Buddy, also crying.

At last, it was time to go. "Bye, guys. I'll miss you. I really will," said Buddy, crying and skipping off to meet his destiny.

All of Buddy's animal friends waved as he skipped by them, heading off into the unknown. "Bye, Buddy!" they called.

"Bye, lovable woodland animals!" he called back. A while later, Buddy was sitting on an ice floe, drifting along the cold sea through a freezing haze, making the transition from the magic land of the North Pole to the real world.

Next there was a massive snowfield to cross. With each exhausting step he took, he sank down five feet. Buddy struggled through it, on and on and on, with no end in sight. His beard was crusted with ice. Finally, utterly spent, he considered leaving himself for dead. But with his last ounce of strength, he pulled out the old photo of his father. Walter Hobbs.

Christmas-Gram for Walter

At that moment, Walter Hobbs sat at the big, polished desk in his spacious office at Greenway Press, a large, children's storybook publishing company. He looked much as he did in Buddy's picture, only a little older and a little meaner.

In front of Walter's desk stood a nun. "You're taking the books back?" she was saying.

"Listen, don't try to make me feel bad here," said Walter. "In actuality, it was you who didn't make the payments."

"We're trying to get you the money, but it's been difficult to raise the funding. The children are sponsoring another bake sale next month. That should help."

"See, there's your problem," he told her. "You can't expect a bake sale to make solid cash these days. You got places expanding their product base with alternative breakfast and dessert items. You guys really need to start thinking outside the box. Do you understand, Sister Peters?"

"The kids really love the books," said the nun, begging now.

"I know that," said Walter, unmoved. "I made them. I'm the one who ran the focus groups."

Deb, his secretary, poked her head in the doorway. "Mr. Hobbs, your two o'clock is here," she said.

Walter looked irritated. "Would you please use the intercom?" he said. "We talked about this."

"Do you want me to use it now? I mean, I already told you."

Walter purposefully ignored her, until she got the message. She backed out of his office, and in a minute her voice could be heard on the intercom: "Mr. Hobbs, your two o'clock is here."

Walter hit the button on the intercom. "Two? Got it," he said into the speaker.

He turned back to the nun. "Tell you what," he said in a compassionate tone. "I know how much these books mean to your kids . . . " He paused, thinking it over. "It's Christmas, what the hell?" he said finally. "I'll give you a three-week extension."

"Bless your heart," said the nun sarcastically.

"Yeah, yours as well," he said, not noticing her tone. "If I were you, I'd stay away from perishable goods. Think consumer services. That's hot right now."

Buddy was now in Canada, halfway there. Now definitely in the real world, he walked through a choppy, muddy, snowy landscape, past a rusted propane tank. A real live raccoon crossed his path.

"Heyyyy! What's your name? I'm Buddy!" he said, expecting the greeting he would have gotten from one of his animated friends.

The raccoon ignored him, confusing Buddy, who cornered it, trapping it as he tried to make friends. The raccoon hissed viciously, but Buddy was undeterred. "Sounds like someone needs a hug!" he said. He lunged at the animal to give it a hug.

Like lightning, the raccoon bit Buddy in the face.

"NUT CRACKERS!!!!" howled Buddy as the raccoon scampered off.

Buddy kept walking, holding his aching face. After a while he found himself walking along a frightening, noisy highway. He looked up, and then stopped in his tracks. NEW YORK CITY/LINCOLN TUNNEL, read the big sign above him. His eyes lit up.

The next part wasn't so easy, however. Buddy timidly inched his way through the Lincoln Tunnel along the walkway, pressing up against the wall while the traffic roared by.

Finally, he was out of the tunnel, but not out of danger. Like a stray cat, Buddy dodged through traffic, his feelings of wonder starting to be replaced with fear. But then, all of a sudden, there it was: the towering skyline of New York City, with the sun breaking over it. He looked at the Empire State Building, then looked at his snow globe. "Whoa . . . " he murmured, awestruck.

Gradually he began getting his bearings on the busy streets, becoming caught up in the rhythms of the city. Every mundane detail of this new world filled him with amazement: the traffic lights blinking in Christmas colors; the steam blasting from the manholes; the scaffolding upon which fearless workers perched high above the crowds.

In Times Square there was a sea of people on the sidewalks. Buddy attempted to greet them all. But to the seen-it-all-done-it-all New Yorkers, he was just another guy in an elf suit. They ignored him.

"Hi!" he said to one passerby. No response.

"Happy afternoon!" he tried with the next. Nothing.

"Salutations!" That one definitely didn't work.

At the corner of Forty-third Street and Seventh Avenue, a man was trying to hail a cab, waving energetically. Buddy waved back. He did not want to be his friend.

Oh, well, no time to be sad about it, because there was so much to look at, like the huge animated billboard high up on the building in front of him. As Buddy stood and gawked at it, a man bumped into him. "Why don't you watch yourself, buddy?" said the man. Buddy wondered to himself, how did he know my name?

Then there was the joy of the revolving door. Buddy went around and around in it until he was wonderfully dizzy.

He knew he had found a special place when he came to the door of a diner that had a sign reading, "WORLD'S BEST CUP OF COFFEE!" He could hardly contain his excitement. Who would have imagined that this dingy, filthy place would have found the answer? He hurried inside. "Wow! The world's best cup of coffee," he gushed to the bored, underpaid staff. "You did it! Congratulations to all of you!" They just stared blankly at him.

Out on the street once more, Buddy looked down and noticed a wad of gum on the ground. Yum! He picked it up, played with it, and then popped it into his mouth. For a moment he chewed it with a smile, thrilled at his luck. Then his face suddenly changed. Oops—forgot the rule Santa had told him.

After recovering from this unpleasantness, Buddy noticed a dog walker using a piece of newspaper to pick up after his dog. Then he saw a way to be extra-helpful. Seeing a pile of poo left on the sidewalk by another dog, Buddy grabbed some more newspaper, picked it up, walked up right behind the man, and offered it to him.

When the man was done yelling at him, Buddy wasn't sure what to do next. He stood on the sidewalk trying to figure it out. But then, what should he see, right smack in front of him, but the Empire State Building! Buddy held up his Empire State Building snow globe and compared the skyscraper before him with his toy one. Yep, this was really it!

"Dad," said Buddy to himself.

Upstairs, Walter Hobbs was in his office. He held in his hands a book titled *The Puppy and the Pigeon*. With Walter was a man from the printing company.

"A reprint?" Walter was saying. "Do you know how much that's gonna cost?"

"Two whole pages are missing," said the printer. "The story makes no sense."

"You think a kid is going to notice two pages?" Walter countered. "All they do is look at the pictures."

In the lobby, Buddy got into the elevator with a bunch of conservatively dressed businesspeople.

He was whistling loudly and happily, which was confusing to them.

Another passenger got on. This one was definitely an accountant. "Can you press sixty-seven, please?" he asked Buddy, who was beside the button panel.

Unsure of what would happen, Buddy pushed 67. The number lit up. "Hey, that's pretty!" he said. Delirious with joy, he pressed all seventy-five of the buttons. "Look at that!" he cried.

As the elevator doors opened and closed, floor by floor, no one was smiling except for Buddy.

Walter and the printer were still at it upstairs.

"How did this happen, anyway?" Walter demanded.

"Well, you signed off on the final plates, and—"

Walter cut him off. "You know what? I don't need to know. Let's just get this solved."

Buddy got off the elevator and found himself in the reception area of Greenway Press. Large reproductions of book covers lined the walls, with titles like *Max the Big Blue Cat* and *The*

Adventures of the Rabbit Gang and Pop. This place looked as if it ran like a well-oiled machine.

Deb was at the reception desk. She looked at the elf, who had appeared in front of her desk. She did not bat an eye.

"Buddy the Elf here for a Mr. Walter Hobbs, please," said Buddy.

"You look hilarious. Who sent you?" Deb asked him.

"Papa Elf, from the North Pole."

"Papa Elf? That's rich." Deb laughed.

In Walter's office, the discussion was ongoing.

"You really think we should ship them?" the printer asked incredulously.

"No," said Walter sarcastically. "I want to take a thirty-thousand dollar bath so some kid understands what happened to a puppy and a pigeon." He took a moment to calm down. "Just ship them!" he ordered.

Deb's voice came over the intercom. "Mr. Hobbs, it's me on the intercom," she said.

"Go ahead," said Walter.

"I think someone sent you a Christmas-Gram."

"A Christmas-Gram?" Walter repeated. "I don't have time for a Christmas-Gram."

Sensing that someone was standing behind him, Walter slowly turned around.

"Dad?" said Buddy. Nervous and excited, he adjusted his hat and vest.

Walter wasn't really listening. "Oh, um, all right, let's get this over with," he said.

By now, a small crowd of people had gathered by the door to watch the supposed singing telegram.

"I walked all day and night to find you," said Buddy.

Walter played along to speed things up. "Looks like you came from the North Pole," he said.

"That's exactly where I came from," said Buddy in surprise. "Santa must have called you."

"Yeah, I just got off my cell with him. So? Go on."

"Go on with what?" Buddy asked.

"Are you gonna sing a song or something, or can I get back to work?"

Buddy was thoroughly confused, but he rolled with it. "A song? Anything for you, Dad. Let's see . . . " He'd never made up a song, but he was willing to give it a try.

"I'm here with my dad," he sang tunelessly. "I've never met him, and he wants me to sing a song. I was adopted, and you didn't know I was born. But I'm here and I love you, Dad!" He gave Walter a big hug.

Walter was perplexed. "Wow. That was weird," he said. "Usually you guys just put my name into 'Jingle Bells' or something."

"It's me, your son!" cried Buddy. "Susan Welles had me and didn't tell you, but now here I am! It's me, Buddy!"

Walter stiffened. "Susan Welles? Did you just say Susan Welles? Who sent this Christmas-Gram?"

"What's a Christmas-Gram?" said Buddy.

"Deb, we may want to call security," Walter whispered.

"I already did," Deb whispered back.

Buddy leaned in toward them, joining in the game. "I like to whisper, too," he whispered.

Five minutes later, Buddy was being rather roughly escorted by two security guards out the front doors and onto the sidewalk.

"My dad runs this whole company!" Buddy told them enthusiastically. "I bet he's a genius."

"Must run in the family," said one of the guards. They both laughed. "I wouldn't come back for a while if I were you."

"Yeah, it seemed like he might need some 'Daddy time,'" Buddy agreed. The guards frog-marched him a little faster. "You guys are strong!" he said.

"Now be a good little elf and go back to Santa Land," said one of the guards.

"Yeah, go back to Gimbel's," chuckled the other one as they pitched him out onto the street.

"Bye, Glenn, bye, Chris!" Buddy called after them.

Elf Heaven

Buddy got to his feet, picked up his elf hat, and dusted it off. Then he looked across the street. There it was. Gimbel's department store— Christmas at its grandest. It was a huge building, decked with dazzling lights and bursting with holiday music. Gimbel's was elf heaven.

"Wow!" said Buddy, his face aglow. He started skipping across the street toward Gimbel's.

BAM! A cab came out of nowhere and hit him! (At least, it seemed to Buddy as if it had come out of nowhere, since he'd been too clueless to look before he crossed the street.) Buddy went flying through the air as traffic screeched to a stop.

Seconds later, Buddy came skipping back. "I'm okay! Thank you!" he said to nobody in particular. Then he continued skipping over to Gimbel's.

Inside the store, the halls were fully decked.

The store had gone all out to create an epic Christmas display. Buddy walked down the aisles, happy as could be in his elf suit.

At the perfume counter, a salesgirl approached him. "Passion fruit spray?" she offered.

"Fruit spray? For real?" asked Buddy. This was great. He opened his mouth and closed his eyes, ready for a shot of wonderful fruit spray. The clerk just stared at him.

"Ready when you are!" said Buddy, mouth open.

The clerk looked around, and then, mildly curious about how this guy in the elf suit would react, sprayed it into his mouth like breath spray: PSSST.

"Yulch!" Buddy stumbled around blindly, scraping his tongue off, about to throw up.

When he had recovered, he resumed his exploration of Gimbel's. Soon he found himself at the bottom of the escalator. What the heck was this? He stood there, afraid to get on, like a kid at the edge of a diving board. Behind him, the holiday shopping crowd was building up and people were getting impatient.

"Are you going or what?" asked an annoyed man behind him.

"Um, yeah . . ." said Buddy uncertainly.

It was now or never. Buddy stepped forward, putting one leg on the escalator. Immediately, the moving stairs yanked him into the splits. "Jiminy Christmas!" he hollered.

Buddy had made it to the second floor alive. Next, he went looking for a bathroom. When he found it, he was absolutely amazed. "Have you seen this toilet?" he said to a stranger as he left the stall. "It's GI-NORMOUS!" Not noticing the look he got from the man, he accosted a second patron. "Look at this toilet!" he said. The man fled.

After Buddy had cleared out the bathroom, he went looking for more fun. And he found it, too, in lots of places. In the candy department, he tried stuffing three thousand candy canes into his mouth at once. Then Buddy climbed in the elevator, where he stood face-to-face with a man, who got very red in the face, for some reason. "You think you're pretty smart, huh?" said the man, and Buddy replied modestly to the compliment, "I'm not that smart, but thanks."

On the first floor was the lingerie department, full of wonderful stuff. "FOR THAT SPECIAL SOMEONE," read the sign.

Buddy picked something up from the counter. "For that special someone? Hmmm . . ." he said to himself.

Just then, a scowling man walked over to Buddy. Buddy didn't know it, but he was the manager of the store elves.

"Man, what in the hell are you doing fartin' around on the first floor?" demanded the man.

"Looking at shiny things!" said Buddy.

"Shiny things? Get back up to the ninth floor!"

"Okay," said Buddy. Why he needed to go to the ninth floor, he did not know, but the man certainly seemed sure of it.

On the ninth floor was Santa Land. As Santa Lands go, it was not very impressive. In fact, it was pretty lame. Buddy inspected it thoroughly.

"This snow looks fake," he told the manager.

The manager could not have cared less. "It's white, ain't it?"

"Snow doesn't just pile up unless it's moved through the use of a tool, such as a shovel," Buddy persisted. "I would give this some natural erosion, a slight wind-drift look."

"What the hell are you talkin' about, erosion? Don't touch the damn snow. What are you smiling at? You think I'm a joke?"

"Oh, no, I'm just smiling," Buddy said. "Smiling is my favorite."

"Well, take it down a notch."

Buddy tried to frown for a second, but his lips quivered and hurt and soon he was smiling again, making the exact same face.

"All right, Smiley, sweep the tinfoil off this path," said the manager. "Santa's going to be here at nine a.m. sharp."

"SANTA?" Buddy's eyes widened. But then he suddenly got skeptical. It was too good to be true. "Wait. Santa Claus?" he said.

"Yeah," said the manager. "Where have you been?"

"The North Pole," said Buddy.

The manager just shot him a disgusted look. "Ha. Ha. Start elfing," he said. "And don't touch the snow." He walked off, looking back in annoyance at this lame-brained new elf.

Now something else grabbed Buddy's full attention. It was a girl—a beautiful, petite girl, dressed as an elf. Her name was Jovie Davis. Like a vision, she glided up to the Christmas tree, climbed a ladder, and began hanging balls. Buddy stared up at her.

"Are you enjoying the view?" she asked him.

"Yes, I am!" said Buddy. "I was standing over there and I thought you looked pretty so I came over here to tell you that you look pretty."

Jovie was suspicious. "Why're you messin' with me? Did Krumpet put you up to this?"

"I'm not messing with you. It's nice to meet a human who shares my affinity for elf culture."

"I wouldn't call it an affinity. I'm just trying to get through the holidays."

Buddy was shocked. "Get through? Christmas is the greatest day in the whole wide world!"

"Well, someone's been drinking the punch," she said. Buddy didn't get it at all, but she didn't notice. "Believe me, after a few years of this, you'll learn to tune it all out," she added.

"Uh-oh. It sounds like someone needs to sing a Christmas carol!" Buddy said.

Now Jovie was really confused. "Are you serious?" she asked him.

"The best way to spread Christmas cheer is singing loud for all to hear," Buddy recited.

"Well, thanks, but I don't sing."

"Oh, it's easy!" Buddy told her. "It's just like talking, only louder and longer and you move it up and down."

"Well, I can sing. I just don't sing. Especially in front of other people. I could never do that."

"Never? If you can sing by yourself, you can sing anytime—there's no difference."

"Actually, there's a big difference," she said.

"No, there isn't," said Buddy. "Watch." He suddenly burst into loud and awful song: "I'M IN A STORE AND I'M SINGING! PEOPLE ARE HERE AND I'M IN A STORE!"

He was beginning to attract stares, and Jovie was looking a little uncomfortable. But Buddy didn't notice; he was finishing his song. "THE STORE IS ALL SHINY AND I'M IN A STORE!!!"

Pleased with his demonstration, he returned to his normal voice. "See?" he said to her.

"Wow," said Jovie, bewildered.

Now a voice came over the store loudspeaker. "Attention," it said, "Gimbel's will be closing in ten minutes. Please make your final purchases."

All the elves looked relieved. Their day was over.

"Dismissed," said Jovie with satisfaction.

Buddy could not believe what was happening. "You're leaving?" he said. "But Santa's coming."

She laughed at his joke. "Yeah, I'll see you tomorrow, um, what's your name?"

"Buddy."

"I'm Jovie," she said. "See ya."

With that, Jovie walked off. Buddy looked around as the half-baked Santa Land emptied out. The doors were locked, the store's employees streamed toward the exits, the lights flickered off.

But Buddy did not leave. Buddy had found a place to spend the night.

Two hours later, a security guard was making his way down an aisle in the toy department. Behind him, Buddy did a commando-style roll through the aisle, and then popped up next to a display of toys. He started pulling all sorts of things off of the shelves: paint, robots, a fire truck. He looked at a logo on one of the boxes. "They have elves in Taiwan?" he wondered aloud.

Uptown, on the ritzy East Side, it was dinner-time at Walter Hobbs's house. His wife, Emily, had prepared a beautiful meal. As Walter filled his plate, their ten-year-old son, Michael, ate without enthusiasm, as detached as possible from the proceedings.

"I'm gonna go eat in my den, okay?" Walter said to his wife. "I've got a bunch of stuff to go over."

"Are you sure?" said Emily.

"Yeah, I'm way behind on a bunch of stuff," he replied. He bent down to kiss her on the forehead, but she didn't offer it, so he kissed the top of her hair instead.

As soon as he was gone, Michael asked his mother, "Can I eat in my room?"

"No," she said.

"Why not? Dad's eating in his den." His voice took on a smart-ass tone. "I have a bunch of homework to go over . . . I'm way behind on a bunch of stuff," he said in perfect imitation of his father.

"You're eating here," she repeated.

"Fine. But I'm not going to talk," said Michael.

"Yes, you are. You're going to tell me how your day was." She waited a moment. "How was your day?" she inquired.

Michael stayed tight-lipped, which infuriated his mother. "HOW WAS YOUR DAY?" she suddenly barked at him.

"It was fine! Okay?"

Later that evening, Walter was looking at his old City College yearbook. He studied a black-and-white photo that showed himself and a young, beautiful woman. It was Susan Welles. Young Walter was wearing a turtleneck and was picking at a guitar. Susan was a little more of a hippie. They both looked enchanted.

Emily entered the room. "What are you looking at?" she asked him.

Walter hastily closed the book. "Nothing," he said. "It's for work."

"You know, it'd be nice if we ate together as a family once in a while," she said.

"I'm sorry, I've gotta work. How do you think I feel—you think I like to work?" he asked.

"Actually, I do." She hesitated, then said what was on her mind. "I'm really worried about Michael. He's getting detached and cynical. They're not supposed to do that until they're teenagers."

"Well, he is thirteen years old," responded Walter.

"He's ten!" Emily corrected him, exasperated. "I don't know what's going on with you, but I've just about had it."

"Had it with what?" Walter asked. That was the wrong answer. He could tell by how she was turning on her heel and leaving the room.

"Emily. Wait," he said. "I'm sorry, I've been under a lot of stress at work."

"If you say the word work one more time, you're sleeping at a hotel."

Walter tried turning on the tiny ounce of charm he had at his disposal. "The chicken thing was delicious," he said.

"It wasn't a chicken thing. It was salmon, zucchini, string beans, carrots, cherry tomatoes, asparagus, mushrooms, and olives."

"Well, it was good," he said.

This conversation was not going well.

In Santa Land, Buddy was just finishing his decorating. He stood back to admire his handiwork.

No Santa Land had ever looked more beautiful. The most expensive merchandise had been used as bricks and mortar. A huge sign embellished with glitter read: WELCOME SANTA! LOVE, BUDDY!!!

Now, off in the distance, Buddy could hear a faint sound. It was the voice of an angel singing. Buddy perked up, cocking his ear. Slowly he rose to his feet; as if following a butterfly, he meandered through the deserted aisles, more and more hypnotized as the angelic singing got louder and louder and clearer and more beautiful.

Finally Buddy pushed through the bathroom door, totally consumed by the greatest voice in the world.

In the bathroom, Jovie stood, singing one part of the classic duet "Baby It's Cold Outside." Buddy was hypnotized. Quietly he joined in, singing the accompaniment part of the duet to himself. But eventually, he couldn't help himself, and began belting out the chorus.

Jovie turned and when she saw Buddy.

"AAAAAHHHHH!" she screamed.

"AAAAAHHHHH!" screamed Buddy, as scared as she was. He bolted off like a jackrabbit, leaving Jovie unsure of what had just happened.

It was a busy Manhattan morning. Walter was going to work. He passed a festive window display that showed a Christmas scene. Buddy was curled up in the fake snow, asleep. His mouth was open and drooling, and he was sweaty from the sun.

Walter kept walking, and then stopped. Was it? He looked again.

Now Walter squinted through the window. It was him. Buddy scratched himself, and then awakened to the sight of his staring father.

"Dad!" Buddy cried, pounding hard on the window, trapped like a tiger. His voice was muffled outside. "DAAAAAAAAAAAAAAAAD!" he yelled.

Walter took off.

It's a Boy

An hour later, Buddy skipped past the security guards in the lobby of Walter's building. He carried a box in his arms. Caught by surprise, the guards had to lunge to grab him.

"HEY!" shouted one of them.

"HEY!" Buddy yelled back. These guys were fun! "Hi, Glenn. Hi Chris! I just want to give my dad this present. I think he's mad at me . . . But he won't be after this."

"You'd better leave that with us," said Glenn.

"Yeah, he's real busy," said Chris.

"Oh, okay. Well, please tell him it's from me, and that I love him so much, and that he's the greatest dad in the world, and that I love him. Okay?"

"Okay," said Glenn, trying to keep a straight face.

That errand done, Buddy went back to Gimbel's, where his new, transformed Santa Land awaited him. His face glowed with satisfaction as he surveyed his work.

It wasn't just Buddy who liked it, either. The place was a smash hit. The shoppers were ecstatic. "Look at that!" they whispered to one another. "Can you believe it?"

Only the manager was grumpy today. "Who took a dump in Housewares?" he growled at one of the workers.

Jovie walked up to Buddy. "Hey, I want to talk to you," she said.

Buddy was now terrified by her, since the incident in the bathroom. "Oh, uh, um, okay, uh . . . " he jabbered. She let him squirm, offering no help. "What do you want to talk about?" he managed to say.

"What the hell do you think?" she replied.

"I know a pig who can run eleven miles an hour," said Buddy brightly.

Jovie was not letting him change the subject. "Why were you in the women's room?" she demanded.

"I heard you singing," Buddy said sheepishly.

"Singing? Right." She looked at him, trying to figure him out. "What were you doing here so early in the morning?"

"Making this," he said, pointing to the dazzling Santa Land.

"You made this?"

"Yes," Buddy said simply. "Why were you here?"

"They turned my water off," she said. She continued studying him. "You were standing there with your eyes closed. What is that, some kind of thing you do?"

Buddy looked at the floor, and then right into her eyes. "You have the most beautiful voice in the whole world," he said.

Jovie could not help herself. His innocence was contagious. "You really were just listening to me, weren't you?" she asked him sincerely.

"I'm sorry," Buddy said.

The manager approached them, and the moment was over. "This is Santa Land, not stand-around-and-wear-pointy-shoes land," he yelled. "Get busy, Santa's here."

Buddy's eyes widened. "SANTA?! SANTA IS HERE?" Looking past the manager, he glimpsed

Santa's back entering a closed-off gazebo. Children were already crowded around to await their turn on his lap.

"Santa!" yelled Buddy, beside himself with joy. He rushed through the crowd toward Santa, his eyes wide and breathless with excitement. When he had almost reached the gazebo, he paused to brush off his uniform and straighten his cap. He was going to see the Big Guy himself! "Santa, it's me! Buddy!" he cried, sliding open the curtain.

Inside the gazebo, surrounded by cheering kids, was a man dressed as Santa. Buddy's smile dropped. "Who the heck are you?" he said.

"Why, I'm Santa Claus," said the man.

"Are not!"

"Well, of course I am. Ho Ho Ho!" the man demonstrated.

Buddy was furious. "If you're Santa, then tell me: What song did I sing you for your birthday this year?"

"Why, you sang, uh . . . 'Happy Birthday'?" tried the store Santa.

Rats! Bad question! Buddy turned to the kids. "He's right," he admitted helplessly.

Santa, the winner by a knockout, strutted past Buddy to his chair. "Why don't you cool it, zippy," he said to Buddy under his breath. To the kids, he said, "Ho Ho Ho!"

Buddy continued to regard this humbug Santa with narrowed eyes. The voice was wrong, the smell was wrong . . . "You're lying! I know it!" he finally burst out. He leaped at the man, grabbing his beard. Off it came. Buddy looked at the beard in shock, as if he were in a horror movie. "AAAHHHH!" he screamed. "His beard is fake! Impostor! He's an impostor! Come on, kids, get him!"

The kids all piled on, wrestling Santa to the ground, loving it. Now the manager dove in and tried to help. In a panic, some of the parents and other elves tried to contain the disaster.

Jovie stood across the room, giggling. She was confused but intrigued by this mysterious elf stranger.

Walter sat behind his desk, staring at the note that accompanied the package that had come from Buddy. The package sat on his desk, still wrapped in a Gimbel's box. The note read, "Dad, this is for you because you are my special someone."

With a certain amount of misgiving, he unwrapped the gift. In the box was a red slinky nightie, with patches of fur in strategic places. He held it up.

In walked Deb. "Hey, the—what's that?" she said.

Walter scrambled to hide the nightie. "What's what?" he asked innocently.

When she was gone, Walter looked deeper into the box and saw that there was a card . It was the photo of young Walter next to his girlfriend, the one Papa Elf had given Buddy. On the other side of the card was a crayon drawing of Buddy.

Deb's voice came through the intercom. "Walter, the police are on line one," she said.

Walter was confused. "The police?" He grabbed the phone. "Hello?" he said. "My son? Michael? Is he okay?" He listened to the voice on the other end. "An elf?" he said. "He's not my—you know what? Keep him there, I'll be right down."

Deb peeked in again. "What's going on?" she asked.

"Nothing," Walter told her. "I need to go." He stood up. "I need to swing by my apartment real quick," he lied. "They're delivering . . . a chair."

"A police chair?" she asked sarcastically.

"It's a regular chair, okay? Cancel my appointments."

Sitting on a cot in his scary jail cell, Buddy looked around woefully. Everything was cold and hard and ugly and mean. He started to cry, sticking his face into the pillow and bawling.

The hardened convict who shared his cell stared at Buddy with disgust. But, like Buddy's innocence, his misery was contagious. After a little while, the convict started crying, too.

The cell door clanged open. There stood Walter.

"DAD!" cried Buddy. He wiped his tears and rubbed his face, trying to look like a good son. The convict wiped his tears away, too, and sat up straight. But he couldn't keep it up, and soon started crying again.

In a few minutes, Walter, having bailed Buddy out, marched out the front doors of the police station. Buddy followed closely behind, almost like a puppy trying to keep up with its owner. Walter had so much to say, he was about to burst with it, but he held back until they were well clear of the station.

"I'm so happy!" Buddy was burbling. "I knew you'd come! I love that you came and I love you, Dad! Know how much I love you?" He spread his arms wide. "This much. Except my arms would have to be way longer, like pterodactyl wings—"

Walter cut him off. "All right, pal, who the heck are you and what's your problem?"

Buddy was confused and injured. "I'm Buddy. Your son."

"I already have a son!"

"Then who am I?" Buddy said.

"Where did you get this picture?" Walter asked him, waving the photo he'd found in the gift box.

"Papa Elf gave it to me."

Walter shook Buddy violently by the lapels, scaring Buddy half to death. "Is this some kind of game?" he shouted. "You want some money!?"

Buddy's lip began to tremble. "I just wanted to meet you . . . and I thought that . . . maybe . . . you might want to meet me . . . "

Walter sensed an element of truth in there somewhere. But he was not convinced. "Sure, who wouldn't want to meet you?" he said sardonically.

"I thought we could make gingerbread houses and eat cookie dough and go ice skating and hold hands."

Walter stood on the sidewalk, conflicted. "Come with me," he said finally.

As they walked down the street, Buddy reached out to hold hands, but Walter's hands stayed firmly in his trench coat. Buddy kept holding his hand out, until Walter suddenly smacked Buddy's hand down in irritation.

Their destination was a pediatrician's office uptown. In the examining room, Buddy sat on the high table as Walter watched.

Buddy reached into a jar of cotton balls and started eating them quickly, one at a time, like cotton candy nuggets.

"Don't eat those," Walter snapped.

Buddy started to eat one more, anyway.

Walter tried to grab his arm, but Buddy merrily faked him out and ate it.

"Am I sick?" he asked Walter as he munched.

"Yes," said Walter, though he did not mean it in the way that Buddy had. "But that's not why we're here. We're here to do a test."

"What kind of a test?"

"A test to find out if you're my son or not."

But distractible Buddy was already on to the next subject. "Why am I sitting on paper?" he asked. He pulled at the roll, and paper spilled out everywhere. The doctor and Walter tried to stop him, but just got tangled up instead.

"So it's clean for each patient who comes in," said the doctor, struggling with the paper. "Try to sit still. I'm going to perform something called a finger prick."

"Finger prick!" repeated Buddy happily. Then his eye fell on the doctor's stethoscope. "Can I listen to your necklace?" he asked.

"No," said the doctor.

"Why?"

"Just sit still." The doctor was getting exasperated.

"Why is there a skeleton on the wall?" Buddy wanted to know.

"I don't know, but there just is," said the doctor through gritted teeth.

"What's his name?" asked Buddy.

"He doesn't have a name!" Walter yelled.

"If I squint, he looks like a pirate flag," said Buddy, squinting.

Meanwhile, the doctor was having problems as Buddy squirmed. "Walter, I can't do this if he's going to keep moving around," he said.

"I'm sorry, Ben," said Walter. "Buddy! Please!"

"He got mad at me," Buddy whispered loudly to Walter.

"Buddy, the sooner you sit still," Walter said, "the sooner we can clear up this horrible mess."

"After this, can we eat sugarplums together?" Buddy asked him.

"Sure! We'll eat sugarplums, and make ginger bread houses, and paint eggs!" Walter said to shut him up.

"That's Easter, not—"

The doctor gave Buddy's finger a tiny prick.

"AAAAAHHHHHHHHHHHHH!!" hollered Buddy.

61

Later, Buddy sat in the waiting room as Walter waited for the results. Buddy held a cotton ball to his finger. Then he ate it.

Next he tapped his finger and turned to a little girl of about seven who was playing with her doll as her mother filled out paperwork with the nurse. "My finger has a heartbeat," he said to the girl.

"It won't hurt so much after a little while," she told him. "What's your name?"

"Buddy."

"I'm Carolyn," she said.

"And what do you want for Christmas?" Buddy asked her.

"A Suzie-Talks-A-Lot."

"I'll put in a good word with the Big Man," Buddy said.

"Thanks. Your costume is pretty."

"Oh, it's not a costume. I'm an elf. Well, I'm a human, technically. But I was raised by elves."

The girl was totally unfazed. "Oh," she said. "I'm a human . . . raised by humans."

"Cool," said Buddy.

Inside the office, the doctor was ready to tell Walter the news.

"Well . . . ?" said Walter.

"Well—" The doctor hesitated. Finally he came out with it. "It's a boy," he said.

The blood drained out of Walter's face. "That's very impossible," he said. He looked as if he was going to faint. "Is that test ever wrong?"

"No."

"No? What am I gonna do? You saw the guy, he's certifiably insane!"

"Walter, I've read about some things that suggest Buddy's behavior isn't necessarily that unusual," said the doctor sympathetically.

"The man skips," said Walter.

"Well, if one was denied a proper childhood, an alternative personality could develop."

"An elf."

"He's probably trying to return to a position of childlike dependency," the doctor explained.

"Okay, so, let's get him some pills or whatever. I'll pay for them—it's not a problem."

"What he really needs is to be nurtured, Walter," said the doctor.

"So, what do you want me to do, breast-feed him?" Walter said grouchily.

"Well, if it were me, I would take him home to meet my family, make him feel I was accessible, that sort of thing. Once he comes to terms with reality, he should move on with his life."

Getting Used to Buddy

That night as Emily was locking up the door to her office and leaving work, she turned to find Walter standing at the bottom of the steps, hands in his pockets, smiling. "What are you doing here?" she asked.

"I was in the neighborhood. I thought I'd walk you home."

"You thought you'd walk me home?" Emily was nonplussed. They begin to walk together. "What, is that so weird?" asked Walter.

"I've worked here for four years. You've never walked me anywhere."

"Well, it's a nice night."

"What's wrong?" asked Emily. She was no dope.

"Why does something have to be wrong? I just said, it's a nice night! I mean, really!" replied Walter defensively.

"Okay, okay, I'm sorry." She took his arm. "Thanks, this is really nice."

"Okay, something's a little wrong," said Walter after a few minutes.

By the time they had gotten home, Emily had begun absorbing Walter's news. "That's . . . well . . . it's wonderful, Walter. You have a son," she said.

"Wonderful. That's one way to put it," he replied.

"Oh, c'mon, this is incredible. It may be a little complicated, but it's nothing we can't handle."

"He thinks he's an elf," Walter said.

"I'm sorry, what?"

"He thinks he's a Christmas elf."

"Oh, I'm sure he doesn't really think—"

Walter swung open the apartment door before she could finish her sentence. Buddy, apparently, had been hard at work. He was nowhere to be seen, but his handiwork was. The place was a recycled winter wonderland. Yards of old garland had been meticulously strung throughout the apartment. Elaborate construction-paper Christmas murals covered the walls. His sense of decorating was impeccable.

Emily just stared, utterly floored.

Meanwhile, in the kitchen, Buddy was scooping globs of frosting into his mouth at a furious pace.

"Buddy?" said Walter as they walked into the kitchen.

Buddy looked up, drooling.

"This is Emily," said Walter.

"Emuree!" said Buddy joyously, his mouth so full that it completely muffled the word. Swallowing the frosting hard, he jumped up and gave her a big hug. "Walter hasn't told me anything about you!" he cried.

Meanwhile, their son, Michael, had come in behind them. "Why is Mom hugging Robin Hood?" he asked.

And so, the Hobbs family began trying to integrate their new elf. At dinner, Walter, Emily, Michael, and Buddy sat around the dining room table eating spaghetti. Buddy had so much to say, it all tumbled out like Niagara Falls.

". . . Then I traveled through the seven levels of the candy cane forest, and past the sea of swirly, twirly gumdrops. And then I walked through the Lincoln Tunnel. Can you pass the soda, please?"

Michael passed him the two-liter bottle, but instead of pouring it into his glass, Buddy chugged the entire thing. The family watched, amazed.

"So, where exactly have you been for the last thirty years?" Emily asked him, trying to make sense of it all.

"The North Pole! He's an 'elf.' That's where elves live!" Walter barked, in a tone that said, "Can't you see the man is insane?"

"He's right," said Buddy cheerfully. "Can you pass the maple syrup, pretty please?"

"I'm sorry," Emily said, "I didn't set out any syrup . . . It's spaghetti."

"That's okay, I'll get it," Buddy offered.

Going into the kitchen, Buddy began sniffing the kitchen cabinets, opened one, and grabbed some syrup. Then he returned to the table and poured lots of it onto his spaghetti.

Walter and Michael shared a disgusted look. It was the first time they'd been in agreement on anything in quite a while.

"You like sugar, huh?" Emily said, smiling.

"Is there sugar in syrup?" Buddy asked.

"Yes," Emily replied.

"Then yes! We elves try to stick to the four basic food groups: candy, candy canes, candy corns, and syrup."

There was a pause. "So," said Emily finally, "will you be staying with us, then?"

"Emily," Walter warned.

"You mean I can stay?" said Buddy.

"Emily!" Walter repeated.

Emily ignored Walter. "Oh, don't be silly, of course you can," she said. "How long do you think you'll be with us?"

"Well, I hadn't really planned it out, but I was thinking, like . . . forever?"

"Emily!" Walter yelled.

"What?" she yelled back.

"May I speak with you in the kitchen for a moment?"

"Um, sure, excuse me, Buddy," she said. They retired to the kitchen to argue.

Left alone, Buddy stared at Michael. Michael ignored him, turning his chair away.

Buddy looked around for a moment. Then he gave forth a burp, but not just any burp. This burp was so loud and long, it was insane.

"Wow. Did you hear that?" said Buddy admiringly.

Michael rolled his eyes.

In the kitchen, Walter was fighting with Emily in hushed tones. "Are you crazy? He can't stay here," Walter was saying.

"Clearly he has some serious issues," she said. "We can't just kick him out into the snow."

"Why not? He loves the snow! He told me fifteen times!"

"Seriously, Walter, he's alone in New York. What's he supposed to do?" she asked.

"Make snow wings, ride the carousel. It's not my problem," he replied.

"Walter, you're his father!"

"Right!" said Walter, storming out of the kitchen.

In the dining room, Buddy and Michael were now sitting in silence. Buddy wasn't sure what to say.

That night, Emily made Buddy as comfortable as possible on the living room couch. It was late. Walter could not wait to get to bed. It had been a long day.

"Good night, Dad," said Buddy.

"Good night," said Walter.

"Tuck me in?"

"What!?" Walter spluttered.

"I can't fall asleep if I'm not tucked in," said Buddy.

"I'm not tucking you in!"

"I promise I'll go right to sleep."

"Fine," said Walter reluctantly. He bent down to tuck Buddy in.

"TICKLE FIGHT!" yelled Buddy, springing up to attack him.

Walter fought him off, really annoyed. "No. Buddy. Stop!" he yelled.

"Sorry," Buddy said.

"Just lie down and go to sleep, okay?"

"Do you want to hear a story?" Buddy asked.

"No. When this light goes off, you are not getting up. Understand?"

"Understand."

Walter flicked the living room light off.

"Dad?"

The light flicked on again. "What?" said Walter.

"I love you."

"Go to sleep," said Walter.

"Do you love me?" said Buddy.

"Yeah, sure. Now go to sleep."

"How much do you love me? Like on a scale from one to ten?"

"Well, I haven't known you for very long, but I would say my feelings are . . . significant."

"Significant," Buddy repeated to himself, satisfied.

"Good night," said Walter.

The light went out for the last time. Walter closed the door. Buddy was alone in the dark. "Dad," called Buddy into the darkness.

There was no response. "Dad?"

Nothing.

"DAD?"

Still nothing.

"DAD?"

There was a long silence.

"DAD!!"

The door suddenly swung open, light shooting into the room.

"WHAT!!" yelled Walter. He was really in a state now.

"Hi," said Buddy.

Walter slammed the door. It was dark again. The footsteps died away.

"Dad?" called Buddy.

In the morning, the kitchen table was set up like a deranged Thanksgiving feast. Buddy had prepared a huge batch of spaghetti. A busy host, he hurried around the kitchen as Emily ate breakfast.

"This sure is something," she said. "I'm usually the one making breakfast."

"Want some more spaghetti?" Buddy asked.

"Um, sure, why not?" she said.

Buddy dumped more spaghetti on her plate, and then sprinkled it with candy Sno-Caps.

"How'd you sleep last night?" she asked.

"Great. I got a full forty minutes and still had time to build that rocking horse."

She followed his gaze to the corner of the room. There she saw a painted and trimmed rocking horse. "My gosh, you built that?" she said. "Where did you get the wood?"

Now she glanced through the kitchen doorway into the living room. The entertainment center had

73

been completely dismantled to provide wood for the rocking horse. Sawdust and paint littered the living room rug.

Now Walter walked into the kitchen, looking flabbergasted. "Why is the TV on the ground?" he asked.

"Good morning, honey," said Emily. She kissed Walter. "Buddy made us breakfast. Isn't that nice?"

Walter looked at the . . . spaghetti? There were so many things to say, but no place to begin . . .

"He packed us lunches, too," said Emily serenely.

There on the counter were three bags of spaghetti, each with a name written in calligraphy.

Emily stood up. "Well, I gotta run," she said. "Thanks for breakfast, Buddy." She grabbed her spaghetti bag. "And the lunch!" she added. She kissed Buddy on the cheek and rushed out of the kitchen.

"Bye, Emily!" Buddy called after her.

Now it was Walter's turn for breakfast. Buddy took a huge spoon and lifted about three pounds of spaghetti into the air. "So, how many scoops?" he asked Walter.

"I'm going to stick with coffee for now," said Walter, looking a little green.

Now Michael staggered into the kitchen, not quite awake. He didn't care to notice the weird food. "I need my allowance," he said a bit awkwardly to his father.

"Did you do the recycling?" Walter asked, equally awkwardly.

"Yeah, I did, okay?"

Walter opened his wallet and peeled off a twenty. Michael immediately shoved it into his pocket.

Buddy was watching all this with interest. "How come you guys don't hug?" he asked. "We always hug in the morning."

"We hugged earlier," Walter lied.

"Yeah, we hugged already," agreed Michael, suddenly his partner in crime. "Bye."

"Bye!" said Buddy.

Walter and Buddy were now alone.

"Listen, Buddy, I wanted to talk to you," Walter said.

"Good, I wanted to talk to you, too," said Buddy. "I've planned out our whole day." He held up an Etch

A Sketch™, on which he had made a list. "First we make snow angels for two hours, then we go ice skating, then we eat a log of cookie dough as fast as we can, and then, to wrap up the day, we snuggle."

"Buddy, I have to go to work," said Walter. "And another thing. If you're going to be staying here, you should think about getting rid of the costume. We've got neighbors and people around here, you know?"

Buddy looked down at himself. "I've worn this my whole life," he said, confused.

"Yeah, well, you're not in the North Pole anymore."

Buddy was unsure. This was big.

"You said you wanted to make me happy, didn't you?" said Walter.

"More than anything," Buddy said.

"Then lose the tights. As soon as possible."

"As soon as possible?"

"As soon as possible," Walter repeated.

"Yes, Papa." Buddy sighed.

Walter turned away from Buddy as he poured himself a cup of coffee. He did not see Buddy removing his yellow tights behind him.

In walked Emily. "I almost forg—" she began, but stopped very short as she took in the sight of Buddy's naked behind.

Walter, meantime, turned back toward Buddy and found himself looking at Buddy getting undressed. He spilled his coffee. "AAAHHHH!!!" yelled Walter.

"AAAHHHH!!!" yelled Buddy, thinking they were playing a game.

Snowball Fight

An hour later, as he walked to work, Walter's cell phone rang.

"Hello, it's Walter," he answered it.

"It worked! It's you!" said Buddy's delighted voice.

"How'd you get this number?" Walter demanded. He was still recovering from this morning, and now here Buddy was again. Was there no place he was safe?

"Emily left an emergency list," said Buddy.

"Is there an emergency?" Walter asked.

"There's a horrible sound coming from the evil box by the window! It sounds like this: EURIEEKCHTH!"

Walter's ear was trashed before he could pull the phone away. "It's not evil. It's the radiator," Walter said. "The heat makes noise when it comes on."

"No, it's not! Wait, yes it is, you were right. Everything's fine."

"I'm hanging up now," said Walter.

"Okay, I love you, I'll call you in five minutes, I love you!"

"You don't need to call me, Buddy, okay?"

"Good idea. You call me," said Buddy.

"Okay. I'm hanging up now—"

"I tuned the piano," Buddy said quickly.

"I'm hanging up now . . ." said Walter.

"I love you . . ."

Walter hung up.

✳ ❄ ✳

Later that day, on the other side of town, Michael's private school was letting out. Michael, in the middle of the crowd of kids streaming out the door, heard something from across the street.

"Michael! Michael!"

He looked over and saw Buddy cutting through traffic.

Michael turned away, embarrassed to death. "Oh man," he said under his breath.

"It's me, your brother!" Buddy yelled, waving his arms. "Hey Michael!"

Kids were starting to notice. The laughing began. Michael absolutely could not bear it. He walked away, ignoring Buddy.

"Michael! Wait up!" shouted Buddy.

Michael could not escape. He was walking home with Buddy.

"Why is your coat so big?" Buddy asked as they walked through Central Park.

"It's a style," said Michael.

"So how was school?" Buddy wanted to know. "Was school fun? Did you get a lot of homework? Do you have a best friend? Does he have a big coat, too? Wanna build a fort?"

Michael finally turned and confronted him. "Leave!" he yelled.

Just then, a snowball whacked Buddy in the head, knocking off his hat. Michael could not help but laugh.

"Ow! Peanut brittle!" howled Buddy in surprise.

THUMP! Now Michael got hit in the shoulder. He stopped laughing. At the edge of a nearby ravine, a big bunch of teenagers was looking down at them.

The best idea was to run, so they did. A barrage of snowballs rained down upon Michael and Buddy as they scrambled behind some rocks. Snow missiles ripped into their barricade.

"Oh, no. These guys are bad news," said Michael. "We better get out of here."

But Buddy was pumped. "We can do this! Make as many snowballs as you can!" he said.

Michael was genuinely worried. "There are too many of them!"

Nonetheless, he quickly formed two snowballs. Meantime, Buddy had already amassed a pile of thirty.

"Ready?" said Buddy.

"Yeah."

Buddy and Michael popped up from behind their cover. Michael threw one snowball and readied another, but was suddenly distracted by the surreal vision of Buddy cradling a pile of snowballs in the crook of his left arm and throwing them, one after another at ungodly speed, with his right.

Buddy's projectiles were a blur as they found their marks. One by one, the bullies were nailed. One of them raised a snowball, and it immediately exploded out of his hand. A stray shot broke off a tree limb. Snowball fights, as it happened, were the one thing Buddy was actually better at than hockey.

Michael watched in awe as Buddy scanned the field for foes. One last remaining bully was cocking his arm back, getting ready to cream Michael. Buddy howled a howl of outrage: "Nooooo!"

As Michael stood frozen with shock, the huge kid wound up and released a snowball right at him. Buddy leaped horizontally, as if in an action movie, and fired a snowball. His aim was precise. It hit the incoming snowball like a Patriot Missile, exploding both of them in midair.

The kid took off, fleeing full-tilt down the path toward a playground a hundred yards away. Watching the running teen, Buddy slowly gathered up a load of snow, packing it into a one last ball. He squinted, then decisively let loose a huge, arcing shot. With expert precision, the snowball hurtled into the diminishing figure, nailing him in the head and sending him sprawling face-first into the snow.

Michael stared at Buddy in awe. "Where did you say you were from?" he said.

Walter was doing some paperwork in his office. He hit the intercom. "Can you bring me in a bottle of water, please?" he asked Deb.

"Fulton Greenway is on his way in," said her voice on the speaker.

Fulton Greenway? The blood immediately drained from Walter's face. "Fulton Greenway? Why didn't you tell me?"

"He just showed up. What size water?"

"When's he coming in?"

"Now," said her voice on the intercom.

"What do you mean now?" He buttoned his suit and checked his reflection in the mirror for nose hairs.

"I mean now," she said. "What size?"

"Hobbs!" barked a dreaded voice.

Fulton Greenway, the terrifying owner of Greenway Press, among other things, walked into Walter's office.

"Fulton! What a great surprise!" gulped Walter.

"I haven't seen you since the retreat. You're looking good," said his boss.

"Thanks, you too. So, to what do I owe the pleasure?"

"Well . . . to be honest, I got a call from my niece," said Greenway.

"Your niece," said Walter, groping for meaning. "I don't think I've met her."

"She's six." Fulton Greenway tossed *The Puppy and the Pigeon* onto Walter's desk.

Uh-oh.

"She wants to know how a certain puppy and a certain pigeon escaped the clutches of a certain evil witch," said Greenway.

Walter vamped desperately. "Believe me, we've already started looking at new printers. This one's obviously gotten sloppy."

Greenway held up the proofs. They had been signed by Walter. "Maybe it isn't the printer who's gotten sloppy," he said.

Walter forced a laugh. "What a disaster, huh? Twenty-five years in publishing, never seen anything like it. Well, I guess you can't bat a thousand, right?"

Fulton Greenway nodded skeptically as Walter squirmed in his seat.

"I got news for you," Greenway said. "Even if those two pages were in there, that book still would have stunk. I read it. I'll tell you, I wish all the pages were missing."

Walter was dying, right there in his chair.

"Have you seen the numbers from this quarter?" said his boss.

"They should be coming in today," Walter choked.

Fulton Greenway held up a sheaf of papers covered with numbers. "They're in," he said.

"That good, huh?"

"*The Puppy and the Pigeon* is tanking hard, Hobbs. My people estimate we'll be posting a minus eight for this quarter."

"Well, we'll bounce back, we always do," Walter tried.

"We're not going to 'bounce back.' We're going to ship a new book in the first quarter."

"The first quarter?" Greenway might as well have said tomorrow.

"I'll be back in town on the twenty-fourth. At that time, I'd love to hear, in great detail, exactly what your plans are for this new book."

"But that's Christmas Eve," Walter protested.

"And?"

"Hey, no problem," Walter said quickly. "It'll be fun to have you in the loop."

Buddy and Michael were at Gimbel's goofing around, playing "gotcha last" amongst the shoppers. They made their way toward the Santa Land that Buddy had built. The sign had been awkwardly changed to WELCOME SANTA! LOVE GIMBEL'S!!!

"I wish Dad were here," said Buddy.

"Why?" Michael asked.

"He's the greatest dad in the world."

"Are you kidding? He's the worst dad in the world. All he does is work," replied Michael.

"Working is fun."

"Not the way he does it. All he cares about is money. He doesn't care about me, he doesn't care about you, he doesn't care about anybody."

"Well, he is on the naughty list," Buddy recalled.

Across Santa Land, standing near a big candy cane, was Jovie. She had looked adorable before, but now she looked seriously adorable.

"You like her?" Michael asked Buddy.

"Like who?" said Buddy.

"The girl you're staring at," replied Michael.

"Um, yes," said Buddy, flustered.

"Why don't you ask her out?"

"Out to where?"

Now Jovie spotted Buddy. She looked over at him and gave him a skeptical wave.

And then she was walking over toward them!

Buddy was visibly flipping out. "We should leave. I need to leave."

"Don't leave!" Michael urged him. "Ask her out!"

"Out?" Buddy repeated.

"On a date, you know, to eat food."

"Food," said Buddy. Jovie had almost reached them now.

"If she says yes, you're in," Michael whispered. "It's like a secret code girls have."

Jovie had reached them. "Well, look who it is," she said.

"Hi, Jovie!" said Buddy. "This is—" But Michael had ditched out. Buddy was on his own.

"That's my brother Michael over there," finished Buddy lamely.

"I was wondering if I'd ever see you again," Jovie said. "So, did Gimbel's give you your job back?"

"No, but it worked out pretty good. They gave me a restraining order."

Jovie looked a little alarmed. "You should really get out of here," she said.

"But I really wanted to see you. You're beautiful, and I feel warm when I'm around you. You make my tongue swell up," Buddy told her.

Jovie was naturally embarrassed. "You are the weirdest guy I've ever met in my life," she said.

"Weird, like, good?"

"I haven't decided," she said.

"So," said Buddy, "do you want to eat food?"

"Do I want to eat food?"

"You know," said Buddy, winking. " . . . the code . . ." Jovie let that slide. "I just took my lunch break," she said.

Buddy was defeated. "Oh. Right. I follow," he said dejectedly.

"But I'm free Thursday night," she added.

A smile slowly broke across Buddy's face. And then, suddenly, he exploded with joy.

"YYEEESSSS!!!" he hollered, pumping the air in an over-the-top gesture of celebration.

When Walter got home from work that night, he found Buddy and Michael hoisting an enormous fourteen-foot-tall Christmas tree up in the corner of the living room. It scraped the ceiling as they wedged it in place.

"What the hell is that?" Walter said.

"A Christmas tree!" said Michael.

"A Christmas tree?" said Walter.

"Buddy chopped it down in the park!" Michael reported.

Buddy smiled at Walter. Walter did not smile back.

Five minutes later, Walter and Emily were in the middle of a heated discussion in the bedroom. "I don't know what you're so worked up about, they're just having a little fun," Emily was saying.

"Fun? Felonies are fun now? I thought felonies were felonies!"

"Okay, the tree thing was bad," she allowed. "We'll have to plant another one. But at least

Michael's happy for once. It's amazing what a little attention will do."

"What's that supposed to mean?" asked Walter.

"It's no secret you haven't exactly been there for him lately. He's a kid, Walter. He's a boy, he needs his father."

"Oh! So let's allow a deranged elf-man to raise him!" Walter ranted. "Maybe we could pull Michael out of school so they can have fun committing felonies together!"

Out in the living room, problems were being solved. "How are we gonna put the star on top?" asked Michael as he unwound a spool of Christmas lights.

"I got it!" shouted Buddy. Holding a large gold star, he took a flying leap off the ottoman toward the tree. Unfortunately, he was way off the mark. Sailing past the tree, he crashed into the wall and disappeared behind the sofa.

In the bedroom, Walter jumped. "What was that noise?" he said.

"It sounded like Buddy slamming into the wall and falling behind the couch," said Emily.

"There's no way we're leaving him here alone. He will trash the place. Maybe you should take tomorrow off and, you know, watch him," Walter said.

"I can't just take off work. Tomorrow's my budget meeting."

"Well, I can't stay home. I'm one pitch away from getting fired."

"Why don't you take him to work with you?" Emily suggested.

"Take him to work with me?" asked Walter.

"Yeah, I bet he'd be very helpful."

"What?" Walter said.

Buddy Goes to Work

The next morning, Walter and Buddy stepped out of the elevator at Walter's office. Buddy, sporting a new suit, looked every bit the professional. Except for the hat.

"Hey, Walter," said one of his coworkers in passing.

"Hey, Jack," Walter responded.

"Hello, Jack!" said Buddy.

Another employee nodded to them. "Hey, Sarah," said Walter.

"Hi, Sarah," said Buddy. "I love that purple dress. It's purplie." She looked startled, then continued walking.

"How's it going, Walter?" said another man.

"Hello, Francisco," Walter greeted him.

Buddy was delighted with this. "Francisco! That's fun to say! Francisco!"

When Francisco had moved on, looking confused, Walter leaned toward Buddy. "Could you at least lose that damn hat?" he whispered.

"I like the hat," Buddy said.

Walter just gave him a look.

"I could try," said Buddy, "but I really like it."

When they were safely inside Walter's office, Walter sat down at his cluttered desk. Deb followed him in with his morning cup of coffee.

"Thanks, Deb," he said.

"Good morning, Debra!" said Buddy. "You have a very pretty face! You should be on a Christmas card!"

"Uh, thanks," she said uncertainly.

After she was gone, Buddy grabbed ten different books and immediately decided that each one was boring. Walter watched him.

"Fran-cis-co," said Buddy to himself, practicing.

Walter just shook his head. "We're cutting down on your sugar intake," he said.

"Why is your name on the door?" Buddy asked him.

"I bought that door. My name's there so no one steals it."

"Is that a joke, Dad?"

"Yes."

"This is your office, isn't it?" Buddy said.

"Well, how about that? He's understanding sarcasm."

"So what are we going to build?" Buddy wanted to know.

"This really isn't that kind of work—" Walter began.

The phone rang. Buddy beat Walter to it. "Buddy the Elf! What's your favorite color?" he said, very fast.

Walter reached over, took the phone out of his hand, and hung it up. "Please don't touch anything," he said, peeved. He had a thought. "Listen, Buddy, have you ever seen a mailroom before?" he asked.

"A mailroom? No!" said Buddy excitedly.

"Mail from all over the world gets sorted all in one place! And some of the bins are shiny," said Walter, making it sound as scintillating as possible.

The mailroom was a loud place, filled with yelling voices, loud machinery, and blaring hip-hop.

Scary-looking young guys in baggy jeans were wrapping and unwrapping massive parcels.

Nobody looked up when the elevator dinged open. There stood Buddy, all alone, looking frightened.

The floor manager finally spotted him. "You Buddy?" he said.

Buddy nodded.

"Well, come on out of the elevator, then."

"Okay."

The floor manager led Buddy over to the main work area. "Welcome to the pit," he said.

An enormous bald man and a bald, wiry kid with a neck tattoo stopped their sorting and looked up at Buddy with threatening glares.

"Over here is the trench," the floor manager continued. "All the mail comes out that shooter. You scan and find the floor each piece is moving to. Put her in a canister and shove her up the tube with the same number. Got It?"

"Yeah!" said Buddy. "I like tubes and canisters and numbers. This place reminds me of Santa's workshop . . . except it smells like mushrooms and everyone wants to hurt me."

✳ ❄ ✳

Upstairs in Walter's office, a writer's meeting was going on. Three writers, Eugene, Huskey, and Morris, sat around a table with Walter.

"So, we've got Greenway coming in tomorrow," said Walter. "Where are we at?"

"Well, Huskey and I were brainstorming," said Eugene, "and we came up with a pretty big idea."

"You're going to love this," said Huskey.

"I heard it already, I think it's fantastic," Morris chimed in.

Walter was pleasantly surprised. "Okay, great. Let's hear it," he said.

"Picture this . . . ," said Huskey. He stopped for a long, dramatic pause. "We bring in Miles Finch."

"The Miles Finch?" said Walter.

"The golden ghost," said Eugene excitedly.

"We bring him in," said Huskey.

"He's written more classics than Dr. Seuss," said Morris, breathing heavily. "It may not be easy, but we think it's worth a shot."

"So, let me get this straight," Walter said. "You guys are pitching me the idea of another writer?"

"Yeah," said Eugene proudly.

"Miles Finch," Huskey added.

For a second, Walter looked as if he was about to get angry. But then his expression changed. "I like it," he said.

Downstairs, in the Greenway Press mailroom, Buddy was in his element. He stuffed and launched mail into the tubes with incredible speed and efficiency. No one had ever seen anything like it.

Almost without noticing, Buddy began singing to himself. "On the first day of Christmas, my true love gave to me . . . " he sang.

He felt a stare and caught himself, turning to find himself facing a stone-cold killer glare. It was the enormous bald guy.

"A partridge in a pear tree," the bald guy sang.

Walter and the writers were now huddled around a speakerphone in Walter's office.

"My favorite book of yours has to be Gus's

Pickles," Eugene was saying. "It was existential, yet so accessible."

"It's a thrill just to be talking to you on our speakerphone," said Huskey.

"So what do you think?" Walter said. "Can you fly in tomorrow morning?"

There was a pause, and then Miles Finch's voice came over the speakerphone, mysterious and brilliant: "I'll give you five hours tomorrow, not a minute more."

"Great," said Walter, relieved.

"I'd like a black S-500 to receive me at the airport. I need the interior of that car to be seventy-one degrees," Finch continued.

"We can do that," said Walter.

There was a beep, and then Deb's voice came in over the intercom. "Walter! There's a situation downstairs," she said urgently.

"I'm sorry, what? Hello?" said Miles Finch on the speakerphone.

"Deb, hang up! Miles, stay on!" said Walter in a panic.

"I do not hold. Do not put me on hold," said Finch's voice.

"We have a problem in the mailroom," said Deb over the intercom.

"What's going on?" said Huskey.

Walter pointed to Huskey. "Do not talk!" he commanded. He leaned toward the intercom. "Deb, please hang up!" he said.

"That's it, I'm gone," said Miles Finch.

"MILES, WAIT!" yelled Walter.

There was a dramatic pause. Was Finch gone?

"I'll be there tomorrow," he said at last. There was an outlet of breath from Walter's group. "Seventy-one degrees," Finch added. He hung up with a click.

"Sir," Deb persisted over the intercom, "the mailroom—"

"Okay, okay! I'm going to the stupid mailroom!" shouted Walter, punching the intercom.

When he got there, he found that Buddy's singing had spread like wildfire. The whole mailroom was now singing a beautiful rendition of "The Twelve Days of Christmas." Everyone was circled around, cheering and singing:

"ELEVEN PIPERS PIPING," sang the large bald one.

"TEN LORDS A-LEAPING," sang the one with the neck tattoo.

"NINE LADIES DANCING," sang one man with a lazy-eye.

"EIGHT MAIDS A-MILKING," sang one with a biker's jacket.

"SIX GEESE A-LAYING," sang the one with the spiked collar.

"FIVE GOLDEN RINGS!!!" everyone sang.

Walter stood quietly, watching this display. The workers began to notice him and, one by one, they stopped, until Buddy was left to continue alone.

"ON THE TWELFTH DAY OF CHRISTMAS, MY TRUE LOVE . . . Gave . . . to . . . " he sang, petering out as he noticed that he was singing by himself.

Then he, too, noticed Walter. He smiled. Walter did not.

It was Thursday night, and so Buddy walked up to the buzzer panel beside the front door of a building in Chinatown. He scanned the list until he found the name Jovie Davis.

He pressed the buzzer. *Bzzzttt!* it went, scaring him half to death. He jumped back, only to find himself face-to-face with a terrifying display window full of Chinese roasted ducks, still sporting heads.

Jovie stepped out of her building door. "Why didn't you come up?" she asked him.

"I got scared," he said. He stood there for a minute, taking her in. "You look miraculous," he said.

Jovie smiled. "Miraculous? Thanks."

They started walking. "So what do you feel like doing?" she asked him.

"I have a few ideas," said Buddy.

"Well, I'm up for anything," she said.

"Really?"

"Sure."

In twenty minutes, Jovie sat blindfolded at the counter of a downtown coffee shop as Buddy set a cup of coffee before her. "Don't look," said Buddy. "Just reach out and take a sip."

"What are you doing?" she asked, smiling. She took a sip.

"Well?" he said.

"It tastes like a crappy cup of coffee."

"Ha ha," said Buddy. He removed the blindfold.

"It is a crappy cup of coffee," laughed Jovie.

They continued their journey, walking north until they were midtown. Buddy found a revolving door and ran around and around and around in it, having a huge amount of fun. Jovie watched, a bit perplexed but enjoying the sight of other New Yorkers getting annoyed.

When he was done with the door, Buddy turned his attention elsewhere. "Check out the size of this!" he said, pulling her by the arm toward a pine tree that someone had decorated for Christmas. "Can you believe it?" he said.

"Come with me," said Jovie.

A few minutes later, she was dragging Buddy across the street toward Rockefeller Center. His head swiveled crazily as he searched for lurking cars. "The yellow ones don't stop! The yellow ones don't stop!" he screamed at Jovie.

They made it across the street alive, and then, there it was: the gigantic, dazzling Rockefeller Center tree, lighting up the night.

"Charles Dickens," said Buddy. They shared their first genuine smile.

Then, since they were at Rockefeller Center, they naturally had to visit the ice-skating rink, where they started having silly fun right away. Jovie accidentally slid into Buddy. Buddy bumped her back, and she bumped him back harder. The bumping escalated until she knocked him off of his feet. They got up quickly and they looked into each other's eyes. Buddy abruptly planted a kiss on Jovie's cheek. "Sorry," he said, flustered.

"You missed," she said smiling.

"I missed?"

With that, she leaned in and kissed him right smack on the mouth.

Buddy's heart filled his whole chest.

Finch

The next morning at Greenway Press, Walter and the writers sat in silence, waiting. Walter checked his watch. They waited some more.

"I sure hope that car's seventy-one degrees," Walter fretted.

Walter and the writers continued to wait at the office. They were now up to the nervous hand-wringing stage.

And then, Miles Finch was striding purposefully through the outer office, the Greenway workers parting before him. They were all awestruck. This was epic.

"I should have brought my camera," said Eugene.

Now the man was outside Walter's office. "All right," they heard him say, before he even walked in. "Let's do this."

In he walked. He was four feet tall.

"Miles! Thanks so much for coming!" gushed Walter, recovering quickly from the surprise. Though he was very small, in this business, Finch was a monster. "We're all big fans. I'm Walter—we spoke on the phone."

"Yeah, yeah, great," said Finch. "Let's get the—uh—taken care of so we can get started."

Walter, understanding his meaning, pulled out a manila envelope stuffed with cash and slid it across the table. The three other writers watched it go across, moving their heads as if they were at a tennis match, until Finch stopped it with his hand. He checked the money and tucked it into his vest pocket. "Okay, cool," he said. Then he got right to the point. "So what have you guys got so far?"

"Okay," Huskey began nervously, "well, we were thinking something like this: We open on a young tomato, he's been through some tough times on the farm—"

"No tomatoes," Finch cut in. "Too vulnerable. Kids are already vulnerable."

"That's what we were kind of thinking," said Walter quickly.

"And no farms," Finch went on. "Everyone's pushing small-town rural. Any farm book will just be white noise."

"Okay. Well," said Walter, "we don't have much time. Do you have any ideas?"

"I've got five or six strong starts," Finch said. "I'm sure we can put something very solid together, no problem. There's one idea I'm especially psyched out of my mind about. It's one of those ideas where you're just, like, YES!"

Walter was now jumping out of his skin with joy and excitement. "What is it?" he almost yelled.

"I'll start with the cover, okay?" said Finch. "Picture this: a—"

"Dad!" yelled Buddy's voice, from outside the office.

Walter was still fixed on Finch, waiting for his golden ticket. Finally he snapped out of it as Buddy barged into the office.

"I'm in love! I'm in love! And I don't care who knows it!" Buddy shouted.

"Not now, Buddy," said Walter, not wanting to tear his eyes off Finch. "Why don't you go . . . uh, back to the pit? I'll come visit you later, okay?"

Buddy started to leave, but then he noticed the four-foot-tall Miles Finch. His face lit up. "You didn't tell me you had elves working here!" he said to Walter.

"Boy, you're hilarious, friend," said Finch with an icy stare.

"So what were you saying, Miles?" said Walter, trying to will Buddy's existence away. "Let's get back to the book."

Finch got back on track. "Okay, at the top of the cover is the title, get this, ready? A—"

"Boy, the candy canes here in New York just don't measure up to elf standards, do they?" Buddy asked his new elf pal.

Miles gave him another icy stare. "Gee whiz, we're all laughing our butts off," he said.

Buddy did not pick up on the sarcasm. "Do you guys have an elf hockey league here? I'm just curious."

"Buddy!" Walter barked. "Please, just go in the basement!"

But Finch was way past letting it go now. "Hey, jack weed," he said to Buddy, "I've got houses in Los Angeles, Hawaii, Vail, and Paris, with a seventy-inch plasma screen in each one of them. So I suggest you wipe that smile off your face before I bite it off." He leaned toward Buddy. "You feelin' strong, friend? Call me elf one more time."

Buddy looked at Walter and shrugged. "Boy, he's an angry elf," he said.

That was it for Finch. He leaped at Buddy. Buddy tried to avoid him, but Finch was surprisingly strong, flipping Buddy over the table.

But then, right out of nowhere, Buddy wound up and clocked him in the face. Then he looked at his own fist in horror. "What have I done?" he said.

This gave Finch permission to deliver five quick hockey punches to the face. Buddy was down for the count. Finch stood, victorious, and grabbed his coat.

"All of you can kiss my vertically challenged butt," he said. He took the envelope full of money out of his jacket pocket and pretended to toss it on the table, pump faking, then returned it to his vest pocket and stalked out.

"Miles, wait!" Walter called after the writer.

Buddy was now sitting up, looking dazed. "A South Pole elf," he said to himself in disgust.

Rubbing his chin, he stood up to face his father. "You're really red," he said, looking a little nervous.

"Dammit, Buddy!" Walter exploded. "This time you really did it! Get out of here!"

Buddy was genuinely scared now. "Where do you want me to go?" he said.

"Go anywhere! I don't care if you're crazy. I don't care if you're an elf! I don't care if you're my son! Just stay out of my life!"

That one stung hard. Buddy ran out of the office, upset as he had never been before.

For hours, he walked through the streets of Manhattan, devastated and depressed. He was giving up.

In his office, Walter was stressed. He rubbed his face, pulled his hair out, talked on the phone. He was losing his career, and he also knew he'd hurt Buddy badly.

Emily called him from a phone booth, laden with last-minute Christmas shopping.

"I can't really talk right now," Walter told her.

"Just tell me, how did the pitch go?" she asked.

"It looks like it's gonna be a little later than I thought."

"Don't be too late," she said. "It's Christmas Eve."

"I gotta go, okay?" said Walter.

"Say hi to Buddy."

"Okay," he said despondently.

As Walter was hanging up the phone, his three writers rushed in, all out of breath.

"Walter!" panted Huskey. "Huge news—the cleaning man just found this."

"What is it?" said Walter.

Huskey handed him a black journal, and Walter started flipping through it.

"Miles Finch's notebook!" said Huskey. "He left it in the conference room! There's three great pitches on the first page alone!"

"Plus we've got his doodle-squiggles all over the back cover!" added Morris. "We're not sure what they mean, but they're probably gold!"

"I say we go with the first pitch in there," said Huskey. "It's a slam dunk!"

"I agree, a home run," said Eugene.

Walter was completely focused now. "How much time do we have?" he asked.

Huskey looked at his watch. "Forty-five," he said.

"Let's get some storyboards ready!" said Walter.

In the Hobbs apartment, Buddy stepped out of the closet, wearing his elf suit again. Never before had an elf looked so sad.

He sat down at the table and unfurled a piece of long paper. Dipping a quill pen into a bottle of ink, he began writing in perfect calligraphy.

"I'm sorry I ruined your lives," he wrote, "and crammed eleven cookies into the VCR. I don't belong here. I don't belong anywhere. I will never forget you. Love, Buddy."

Folding the scroll, he set his snow globe down on the crease to hold it.

Then he walked out into the night.

In his elf suit, Buddy trudged through the stormy New York night. The wind blew viciously.

Buddy walked against it, the snow blowing into him. He barely noticed.

When Michael got home, his arms full of presents, he looked around the empty house. "Buddy?" he said.

The Big Guy

At the office, Fulton Greenway sat with the board members at the end of a conference table, looking sharp as a tack. Walter sat at the other end, looking even sharper.

"As you know," said Greenway, "we need a big launch, fast, to get this company back on track. So I think I speak for my fellow board members when I say . . . this better be good."

Walter just smiled, and then rechecked his story boards, beaming. "I'm confident, sir. You will not be disappointed."

"Let's hear it," Greenway said.

"My pleasure. I'll start with the cover, okay? Picture this: a—"

"Dad," Michael's voice interrupted.

Walter turned to find that Michael had entered the conference room. "Michael?" he said.

He blinked, unable to believe his eyes. Then he turned back to Greenway. "So there's this cover—"

Michael did not give up. "Buddy left!" he persisted.

"What?" said Walter.

Michael held up the calligraphy scroll that Buddy had written. Greenway and his team just looked at one another, confused.

"He wrote this note!" Michael said to Walter. "He left his snow globe! He's gone!"

Walter did not know which way to turn. "Okay, listen, let me finish this meeting and we'll figure this out, okay?" he said.

"Finish your meeting?" Michael shouted. "How'd I know you were going to say that?"

He turned to leave, furious. Behind him, Walter was torn. Finally he jumped to his feet. "Michael, wait!" he said.

Michael stopped in his tracks, looking hopeful. Was his father really going to come through, for once?

Walter turned to his boss. "Mr. Greenway, we have to reschedule this," he said.

"We don't have time to reschedule!" growled

Greenway. "I want to hear the damn thing, now."
He turned to Michael. "Son, this has to wait," he
told him.

"Don't tell my son to wait," Walter said. "Can't
we do this some other time, Mr. Greenway?"

"I just flew in to hear this pitch, and I intend to,"
said Greenway.

"Well, it's gonna have to wait,"
Walter countered.

"If you want to have your job when you come
back, you better pitch me that book right now."

Walter and Michael turned around, stormed
through the door, and walked down the hall
triumphantly together, father and son.

"If you walk out, Hobbs, you can never come
back to Greenway!" the boss called out after them.

They kept walking.

Buddy was on the Fifty-ninth Street Bridge,
looking down through the swirling snow at the
water and contemplating the worst of all possible
conclusions. The waves crashed and churned
far below.

At the same time, Walter and Michael were walking quickly toward Central Park, searching, half-jogging, losing hope. Where on earth was Buddy?

Buddy closed his eyes tight. Then he looked up, a tear streaming down his cheek.

Suddenly, something caught his eye: a distant point, with a glowing contrail of smoke streaming out behind it. Buddy narrowed his eyes to get it into focus as it drew nearer. Slowly the shaped resolved itself. It was Santa's sleigh, tangled up with its nine reindeer, fishtailing wildly through the sky. It was going to crash!

"Santa!?" said Buddy.

Walter and Michael were just outside the park. Walter was facing away, so he didn't see the sled plummeting through the sky behind him. Michael, however, saw it all. His face glowed with wonderment.

The sleigh crashed into Central Park.

"Oh . . . my . . ." said Michael.

Walter had missed it, but he heard the sound.

"What was that?" he asked, turning.

But Michael was running toward the park.

Walter took off after him through the woods. "What happened?" he called. "Michael, wait up!"

Meanwhile, Buddy was running frantically toward Santa's sleigh, which he could see in the distance. It had crashed into the Great Lawn, a large, open expanse in the middle of the park.

At the crash site, the reindeer peacefully grazed as Santa struggled with the smoking sled. The landing had been rough; the sleigh had dug a deep, fifty-foot-long trench in the snow and dirt.

Buddy came screeching up to him, but Santa did not see him as he tried desperately to repair the problem, his head hidden under the hood. Smoke rose from the front of the sled .

"Santa!" yelled Buddy.

Santa jumped out from under the hood, clutching a tire iron. "Back off, slick!" he warned. Then he looked harder. "Buddy? Is that you?" he said.

"Are you okay?" panted Buddy.

117

"Boy, am I glad to see you," Santa said. "The Claus-o-Meter suddenly dropped down to zero. There's almost no Christmas Spirit, and the strain was too much. The engine broke free of her mounts. I need an elf's help."

"But I'm not an elf, Santa. I can't do anything right," Buddy tried to explain.

"Buddy, you're more of an elf than anyone I've ever met, and the only one I would have working on my sleigh tonight," said Santa.

"Really?"

"Really. Will you fix it for me, Buddy?"

"I will," said Buddy happily. "Papa taught me how to fix the engine."

"You'll have to find it first," said Santa. "She dropped off the sleigh, back there a ways."

Buddy ran off into the woods.

Down in Chinatown, Jovie walked out of her kitchen as New York 1, the local news channel, droned quietly on the TV. On the screen was a breaking news story from Central Park. A reporter was on the scene, standing before a police barricade. A few dozen people had gathered to watch.

"I'm here in Central Park," the reporter said, "where it is unclear exactly what has happened. What we do know is that authorities have closed the park and are in the process of clearing it. All that people here seem to agree on is that they saw something fall from the sky. I'm here with Mike Stefanopolis, who says he was able to get a firsthand look at what happened. Tell me, Mr. Stefanopolis, what did you actually see?"

She stuck the mike in the face of the witness, who held a small child in his arms. "I was walking along," he said, "and I saw something drop from over there and kind of fall in that area . . ."

"Something? Do you mean a meteor?" said the reporter.

"It wasn't like that. It sounds crazy, but it looked like, um, well, uh. . . " He hesitated, embarrassed.

"It was Santa's sleigh!" said the child.

"Interesting . . . " said the reporter.

The report was now interrupted by the anchorman, breaking in from the studio. "Sorry to interrupt, Charlotte," he said, "but those of you watching at home might be interested to see some New York One exclusive amateur footage that just came in. It might just offer some insight into the park situation."

On the screen appeared a zoomed-in, blurry image of Buddy, running. It closely resembled the classic Bigfoot shots from the 1970s. The footage ended in a freeze-frame of Buddy, looking over his shoulder toward the camera.

Jovie walked back into her kitchen just in time to hear the newsman say, "It seems to be a strange man dressed as an elf."

"Oh my God," she gasped, seeing that it was Buddy.

When they came across a smoking object in the snow, Walter and Michael stopped to look at it. "What the . . . ?" said Walter.

"I don't know," replied Michael.

It was Santa's missing engine.

"You found it!" said a familiar voice.

They looked up, and there was Buddy, loping

toward them. Michael ran to him and hugged him hard. "Buddy!" he cried.

"There's something I've got to tell you guys!" Buddy said in a rush.

"No. Me first," said Walter urgently. "There's something I want to tell you right now. I take back everything I said. You may be a little, how do you say, chemically imbalanced, but you've been right about a lot of things. I promise you, I'm going to be making some changes in my life. I don't want you to leave . . . I need you. You're my son, and I love you."

He hugged Buddy. Buddy was moved beyond words.

"So, what was it you wanted to tell me?" asked Walter.

"What?" said Buddy.

"You had something you wanted to tell me?"

"Oh, right." Buddy led them a short distance, through the trees to the Great Lawn. There was Santa's grounded sleigh, surrounded by nine grazing reindeer. It was an awesome sight, and Walter stared in disbelief.

"Cool," said Michael.

Saving Santa

Some distance away, another man was now being interviewed by the reporter. " . . . and then there was this big, like, dirigible thing with this big tractor beam that lifted me up into the sphincter in the bottom of the mother ship . . ." he was saying.

The reporter was thoroughly confused. "And when did this happen?" she asked.

"Nineteen ninety-six," he said. "In Joshua Tree."

It was clear that the man was deranged, but the reporter, unfazed, continued. "Dick," she said to the anchorman in the studio, "according to authorities, the area has been cleared. Only the Central Park Rangers remain in the park. These forces are highly trained, but rarely see action. Some have accused them of being too 'gung ho' when called into duty—and their controversial crowd control tactics at the Simon and Garfunkel concert in eighty-five are still under investigation."

And indeed, four of them were lined up on horseback along a nearby ridge. Their black mares breathed steam into the cold air as the riders stared silently into the night. The Rangers wore black leather boots and trench coats. Their chrome helmets sat atop faces that were shrouded in shadow. Each rider wore a silver eagle badge that read CENTRAL PARK RANGERS. They looked down upon the sleigh, quite a distance away.

Meanwhile, Jovie was running down the street, heading to Central Park.

While Walter and Michael tried to wake up from this strange dream, Buddy worked on the engine.

"So," Walter said hesitantly to the Big Guy. "You're . . . real?"

Santa did not look up from his work. "Hold this for a sec," he said, indicating the hood.

Stunned, Walter and Michael held the hood up.

"Buddy's really an elf?" Walter asked.

"Actually, I'm adopted," Buddy said.

Michael looked closely at the man in the red suit. "So, you're really Santa Claus?" he said.

"Tell me, what did you want for Christmas, Michael?" Santa asked.

"I wanted a skateboard."

Santa pulled out a scroll. He pointed to Michael's name in calligraphy, and peered closely at the notation beside it. "Not just a skateboard," he said, "a Real Huf board with high 145 Thunder trucks, 52 millimeter Spitfire classic wheels and bolts from Diamond, and some Swiss bearings."

That did it. As of that moment, Walter and Michael both truly believed.

Unnoticed by any of them, the needle on the Claus-o-Meter moved up a little. The sleigh shuddered and rose, then fell back to the ground.

"What happened?" asked Michael.

"You made my sleigh fly," said Santa with a little smile.

"What do you mean?"

"Before our Viper engine days, this thing used to run solely on Christmas Spirit," Santa explained. "You believed in me. You made my sleigh fly."

"Then fly away!" said Michael.

"I'm afraid I need more than the spirit of just two people to reach the sky without the booster engine to help," said Santa.

"Hold it," Michael said. "If you're really Santa, we can just get some news cameras in here and everyone will believe in you. Then your sleigh will fly, right?"

Santa thought about this, but then shook his head. "Christmas Spirit is about believing, not seeing. If the whole world saw me, all would be lost. The paparazzi have been after me for years."

Suddenly, Michael spotted the riders on the crest in the distance. "Look!" he cried.

"Oh no," said Santa. "The Central Park Rangers."

They all looked up in fear as the riders disappeared into the woods, heading toward them.

Buddy pulled Walter aside, and Michael followed them. "Santa needs your help," Buddy said to them.

"But what can we do?" said Michael.

"I got an idea," Buddy said. He whispered his plan to Walter and Michael.

As the Rangers galloped through the darkness toward them, Michael snatched the List out of Santa's hands and ran into the woods.

"My List!" cried Santa. He started to chase Michael, but Buddy stopped him.

"Santa, let him *go*," said Buddy, very sure now of his plan. "You'll get it back."

"Give me your coat and your hat," Walter said to Santa.

"But Mrs. Claus made them for me," said Santa.

"Hurry!" said Walter. "Just think about what would happen to Santa Claus in prison."

Santa was persuaded. He handed over the coat and hat, and Walter donned the oversized ensemble.

The crowd at the police line had swelled to over a hundred. Michael burst out of the park carrying the List, and interrupted the man who was being interviewed by the television reporter. "And they have these long, cold probes—" he was saying.

"It's him!" Michael broke in. "It's the real Santa Claus! His sleigh can't fly 'cause nobody believes in him!"

The reporter stayed focused on the interview. "What exactly did you—" she began, but Michael interrupted again.

"Everyone out there, Santa needs us to believe!" he yelled. "I can prove he's real. This is Santa's List!"

He opened the List and began reading out loud: "Lynn Kessler wants a Powerpuff Girls™ play set. Mark Webber wants an electric guitar . . ."

Lynn and Mark, standing in the crowd, listened with eyes that went wide—believing, giving Santa the power he needed.

In the Hobbs apartment on the East Side, Emily had just walked in the door. Still in her coat, holding bags of groceries, she caught sight of her son on TV. "Michael!" she gasped.

At the same time, Jovie arrived in the park,

making her way in through the back fringes of the crowd just in time to see Michael reading the List to the camera.

"Stan Tobias wants a powerpumper water rifle," he read. "Carolyn Reynolds wants a Suzie-Talks-A-Lot."

Carolyn, the girl from the doctor's office, was at home watching this on TV. "Thank you, Buddy!" she cried.

"Dirk Lawson wants a day of pampering at Burke Williams Spa," Michael read.

In a downtown bar, a rough-looking biker jumped, startled and embarrassed. His biker friends all looked at him strangely. "Must be another Dirk Lawson . . ." mumbled the biker.

"Dave Keckler wants some Nike Sox™!" Michael read.

Now the reporter tried to step in. "That's quite enough, little fella," she said officiously.

"What's your name?" Michael asked her.

"I'm Charlotte Dennon, New York One," she said, smiling her television smile.

"Let me see. D, D, D . . ." said Michael, scanning the List. "Charlotte Dennon wants a Tiffany engagement ring, and for her boyfriend to commit already."

The reporter shut her mouth with a snap, embarrassed.

Meanwhile, on the Great Lawn, the surge in Christmas Spirit had caused the needle on the meter to jump, and Santa's sleigh to rise a foot off the ground.

"We got power!" cried Santa. He snapped the reins, and the sleigh began to lumber forward.

Under the sleigh, Buddy was still struggling with his task. "I don't have the engine fixed yet!" he yelled to Santa.

At the barricade, the reporter still stood speechless, staring at Michael, as the anchorman talked into her earpiece. "Charlotte...? Charlotte...?" he said.

Finally he gave up. "We seem to be having some technical difficulty with our remote unit," he said to the television audience. "Now for weather on the ones."

But Charlotte was still gaping open-mouthed at Michael. The tech crew turned off the lights on the remote unit.

"No! Turn it back on!" cried Michael, knowing that the plan to get the sleigh into the air depended on the cameras and the people watching him at home.

"How did you know that?" Charlotte said, as if talking in her sleep.

"I'm telling you, it's Santa," said Michael. "We have to get the cameras back on! He needs our help!"

Though the scene had gone dark, the crowd had not dispersed. Now they offered scattered boos to the TV crew. "Let the kid read!" someone shouted.

"What do I want?" asked another voice.

Jovie worked her way through the milling crowd. "Where's Buddy?" she asked Michael.

"He's with Santa. The sleigh won't fly. There's no Christmas Spirit. We need to get these cameras back on."

Now Emily arrived, in a panicked rush. "Michael!" she shouted in relief when she saw him.

"Mom!" he cried, running to her throwing his arms around her.

Jovie looked around, her mind working. She was

trying to think of a plan. Then she remembered something. "The best way to spread Christmas cheer is singing loud for all to hear . . ." she repeated to herself.

Walter was standing watch in the Great Lawn near the sleigh, and now he saw something scary: The mounted police were charging them.

"Get out of here!" Walter shouted to Santa. "They're coming! There's enough Christmas Spirit to start the sleigh moving."

Buddy leaped into the sleigh. Slowly it moved forward in a herky-jerky way, hovering a foot off the ground.

The mounted riders came straight at Walter, who was wearing Santa's hat and coat. "Hey! I'm right here!" he yelled, waving his arms and trying to look as much like Santa as possible. "Ho ho ho! You got me! I surrender!"

They rode right past him, following the sleigh, which was swerving past trees, scraping bark, and smashing branches. Over his shoulder, Santa caught a glimpse of the Rangers, who were in hot pursuit.

"Grab the shotgun under the seat and give 'em some heat!" Santa shouted to Buddy.

"What?!" said Buddy, startled.

"It's a joke, Buddy, lighten up!" Santa chuckled. "Listen, there's barely enough magic to make this thing move. Keep working on the engine!"

At the police barricade, Jovie remembered what Buddy had said and found herself inspired by his words. She climbed atop a horse's carriage and looked out over the huge crowd that had gathered. Timidly, she began singing, her sweet voice cracking with fear.

"You better watch out, you better not cry, you better not pout, I'm telling you why . . ." Jovie sang.

Walter, his work as a decoy finished, arrived to join his family just as Jovie began to sing. "He wasn't lying," he said to Emily.

"Merry Christmas," she said. They hugged.

On the sleigh, Buddy was risking his life, working on the engine at high speed. Smoke and sparks billowed out as Santa struggled to maintain control. They hit a bump and some toys flew out of the back. A jack-in-the-box popped open just as it flew past Buddy. "Aaaahhhh!" he screamed.

Now there was a new problem. Dead ahead was a giant fountain, smack in their path. The Rangers were very close behind.

"I've almost got it!" Buddy yelled.

"We need power, now!" Santa shouted back.

Buddy gave the engine one last desperate tweak, and it roared to life. The surge of power blew the sleigh forty feet into the air, clearing the fountain.

"YES!" yelled Buddy in triumph. "I did it! I'm the greatest adopted elf in the whole wide world!"

"Good job, Buddy!" yelled Santa.

But suddenly—trouble. The belly of the coach nailed the winged statue atop the fountain, yanking the whole engine back out of the sleigh, destroying all the work Buddy had done. The engine whirled and shot off into the trees, leaving the engineless sleigh to crash down to the bricks.

"That's it," said Santa. "With no engine, we're toast."

At the barricades, however, Jovie was still

singing her heart out. "He sees you when you're sleeping . . ."

Emily was the first to join in, and then Michael sang too, and then some others.

With its low level of spirit power, the sleigh scraped along the paved mall, sending sparks showering into the night air as the horses closed in.

But at the barricade, the whole crowd had now joined in singing with Jovie. The reporter put her finger to her earpiece. "Dick, come back to Remote Three," she said to the anchorman in the studio. "I think I've got something here."

"He knows if you've been bad or good, so be good for goodness sake," everyone was singing, loudly and clearly now.

The lights went back on, and the cameras started rolling. "Charlotte Dennon, back at Central Park," the reporter said into the camera. "Although it's still unclear what led to this holiday rally, hundreds of New Yorkers seem to have spontaneously gathered together and broken out into song."

All over the city, people were watching the

broadcast and breaking into song along with the crowd in the park: the Greenway mailroom guys, Walter's three writers, Ben the doctor, Carolyn, the little girl from the doctor's office, the guards from the Empire State Building, all singing along in perfect harmony. Even the crew from Gimbel's was singing—except for the manager.

Santa's sleigh was moving, but it was hurtling right into the barricades, with no steering and no lift. They were headed for a collision.

As Emily and Michael sang along, Michael looked up at Walter and noticed something peculiar. "Wait! You're not singing!" he said.

"Yes, I am," said Walter guiltily. He'd been busted by his own kid.

"No, you're not," Michael kept on. "You're just moving your lips!"

"Michael, please, what's the big deal?" Walter said.

"Dad!"

Then, in spite of himself, Walter belted out the chorus in such a loud voice that it drew looks from the singers around him. "Santa Claus is coming to town!" he sang, the bad notes rising into the chilly night air.

Somehow, that was the thing that did the trick. The Claus-o-Meter shot up into the red zone as a dashboard light blinked "HO HO HO." Santa howled in approval. The sleigh flew up into the night air and over the barricade, the reporters, and the onlookers. The Rangers slid to a stop, foiled at last.

As the shadow of the sleigh zipped high over them, the whole crowd joined in, singing their hearts out. Jovie couldn't believe it. She sang louder.

A voice boomed out into the magical winter night. "Ho, Ho, Ho. Merry Christmas!" it said. Then Santa's sleigh whipped down Sixth Avenue and into the Manhattan night sky, silhouetted at last against the moon.

Epilogue

by Papa Elf

And so, with a little help, Buddy managed to save Christmas. And his spirit saved a lot of other people, too. It was quite a Christmas, and quite a New Year, with lots of presents and lots of happiness for the Hobbs family.

Walter started his own independent publishing company. His first book was written by a brand-new, critically acclaimed children's author, named Buddy. The book was called *Elf*—a fictional story about an adopted elf named Buddy, who was raised in the North Pole, went to New York, ate spaghetti, worked in a mailroom, and eventually saved Christmas.

And every year, on Christmas Day, after all the presents are opened by children around the world,

Buddy and his dad make up for lost time. Sometimes they even ice skate together at Rockefeller Center in the middle of the night, even if Walter still doesn't want to hold Buddy's hand. But Walter even made the jump from the Naughty List to the Nice List.

And, as for me, I can't complain. Buddy comes up to visit from time to time, though he does bump his head quite a lot, which makes him say bad words like Yikes and Golly. He comes with his nice young wife, Jovie, and their new baby, Susie. Susie looks very cute in her pink elf hat.

THE END